Cage

THE K9 FILES

Dale Mayer

CAGE: THE K9 FILES, BOOK 27
Beverly Dale Mayer
Valley Publishing Ltd.

Copyright © 2024

ISBN-13: 978-1-778866-02-9
Print Edition

Books in This Series:

Ethan, Book 1

Pierce, Book 2

Zane, Book 3

Blaze, Book 4

Lucas, Book 5

Parker, Book 6

Carter, Book 7

Weston, Book 8

Greyson, Book 9

Rowan, Book 10

Caleb, Book 11

Kurt, Book 12

Tucker, Book 13

Harley, Book 14

Kyron, Book 15

Jenner, Book 16

Rhys, Book 17

Landon, Book 18

Harper, Book 19

Kascius, Book 20

Declan, Book 21

Bauer, Book 22

Delta, Book 23

Conall, Book 24

Baron, Book 25

Walton, Book 26

Cage, Book 27

Trey, Book 28

Boxed Sets and Bundles

https://geni.us/Bundlepage

About This Book

Welcome to the all new K9 Files series reconnecting readers with the unforgettable men from SEALs of Steel in a new series of action packed, page turning romantic suspense that fans have come to expect from USA TODAY Bestselling author Dale Mayer. Pssst... you'll meet other favorite characters from SEALs of Honor and Heroes for Hire too!

Finding a missing K9 dog is a great way to give back to both the people and the animals who have helped Cage over the years. He didn't expect his actions to help someone else— maybe even himself. Yet that's the likely the outcome when he realizes the dog belongs to a little boy who suffers from spina bifida and who lost his parents in a car accident. Now Cage must save a little boy and his dog, who need each other more than ever.

Risa never should have split from Cage years ago, and seeing the man he is now just accents all she has lost. Even harder is the realization that time did not change anything between them. He is still the one for her.

Yet getting to a happy future looks less and less likely, as the two of them realize something sinister underlies this whole mess, and someone doesn't want them to survive …

B ADGER PUT DOWN his phone and looked at Kat. "That turned out better than expected."

"Yeah, but what the hell's wrong with our world, when they go after a dog and end up with some other crazy scenario that none of us could even see coming?"

"I think that's just life," he said, with a nod. "However, you're right. We just barely get things straightened up, and something else goes haywire. You don't have another case now, right?"

"Not so sure about that. ... We still have Timber to deal with."

"Sure, still Timber to deal with, but he will always be somebody we're dealing with," he pointed out. "He's not set up, but I know he's getting closer."

She nodded. "So there just might be something else." Then she pulled out two file folders from among her stack.

"More?"

"I did tell them that we will be enlisting Timber's help down the road with further cases, but they didn't think there should be any more. They've instituted some new changes."

Badger added, "Yet one or two more War Dogs might still be caught up in the old system though."

"But the new changes should help a lot."

"Do we believe them when they say that?" he teased,

with an eye roll. "Besides, you seem to be handling this job just fine."

"Sure, but that doesn't mean I'm ideally suited for this type of work, especially when my development of new prosthetics is really taking off, for humans and animals."

"That's true enough too," Badger agreed, "so where is this first case starting from?"

"Michigan."

"What's going on there?"

"A family with a paralyzed boy adopted the War Dog, but then his parents were killed in a car accident. Unfortunately the boy was put into foster care because he had no relatives ready to step up and take him, and the dog has since disappeared."

"Oh, good Lord," Badger muttered, shaking his head. "That's not good. Every boy needs a dog, and it sounds as if these two need each other."

"If it's the boy's dog, the loss would be very hard on both the boy and the dog," she agreed, "and our job is to find the dog."

"And to sort out whether the boy can get the dog back."

"That can only happen if anybody is willing to take both him and the War Dog," she noted. "Unfortunately, when an entire family gets wiped out like that, the odds aren't great to place both, particularly when they each have disabilities."

Badger shook his head at that. "Tell me that you have somebody in Michigan."

"No, I sure don't." She hesitated.

"But?"

"I might know somebody, but I haven't talked to him for a long time."

"What's his name?"

"Shelton."

He frowned at her. "Cage Shelton?"

"Yeah."

"Why would you think he would be a good fit for this job?" he asked curiously.

She shrugged. "I'll say *instincts*, but also I know that he was raised with dogs. He's ex-military of course," she added, "but, more than that, his younger brother was also in a wheelchair."

Badger gazed at his wife, and a slow smile dawned on his face. "Not the typical matchmaking of a couple, yet I can see the similarities between our case and Cage's life. Plus, you want to help everyone. Just right up your alley, isn't it?"

She shrugged. "Breaks my heart to think that the War Dog bonded to a boy who needed him desperately, and now the boy has lost not only his family but also his dog."

"Yeah, that's not fair, is it? So, what is it you expect Cage to do?" he asked, now curious.

She gave him a bright smile. "Everything, absolutely everything."

"At this point, I expect miracles from every one of our guys," Badger declared.

She laughed. "It doesn't hurt to expect miracles. That doesn't mean they always happen, but, in this case, … I've got a feeling."

CHAPTER 1

CAGE SHELTON ANSWERED the phone with joy in his heart. "Hey, Kat. How're you doing?" he asked, with a beaming smile. "Does this mean you got Jason's new legs in for him to try?"

Kat chuckled. In a smooth, soft tone, she replied, "Not yet. I know I said *any day*, yet it won't be today. I'm still expecting it anytime though."

"Just not today?" Cage could barely keep his disappointment out of his tone. He looked outside, happy that his younger brother was shooting hoops from his wheelchair, happy as a bug, as he always was when he could play outside.

"Yeah, but I was calling about something else. It's a … not really a favor, but maybe it is," she began.

Any hesitation in Kat's voice was unusual, so Cage stated, "Anything for you. You've been there for us every step of the way."

"Hey, Jason is an awesome guy," she noted, with a smile easily coming through her tone of voice. "It's easy to help him. He's always willing to do what's needed."

"Well, you're doing a ton for him, so if I can do something to help pay it back, I'm in."

"Outside of paying the bills, you mean?" she teased.

"The bills just go with the territory," he acknowledged, "and you always go way beyond anything you charge us for."

"Well, I try to help," she murmured. "Do you have any experience with War Dogs?"

He frowned. "War Dogs. That's an interesting question."

"Why?"

"Well, in a way, all us military types have had experience with them because, when we are out there, deployed, they're all around us. I haven't had any training experience, but I've certainly been there with the K9s, and I'm definitely comfortable with them, if that's what you're asking."

"That's partly what I'm asking about," she replied. "I don't know if you've heard anything about some of the work that we've been doing with War Dogs …"

"Working with War Dogs? With … prosthetics?" he asked in confusion.

She laughed. "No, although there is a War Dog that I'll be working with coming up that'll potentially get a prosthetic from me—depending on how I can make the hip socket work."

And knowing that she was about to break into explanations that would completely go over his head, Cage interrupted her. "Whoa, whoa, before you go down that pathway—"

"You know me so well," she admitted, with a sigh.

"At this point, I think I do. The minute anything comes up about your line of work, you get so into it, so intense, that you leave us all in the dust."

"Hardly in the dust," she clarified, chuckling, "and you're definitely no dummy when it comes to this stuff."

"If I'd realized a field in this area could be a profession before I joined the military," he shared, "I probably would have gone into it myself."

"I wish you had," she noted ruefully. "I could really use some help."

"I don't think I have the training and the temperament now."

"Well, you're an engineer, aren't you?"

"I am, and a mechanical one at that, but you need a whole lot more than what I am trained for."

"But you could learn," she stated.

He burst out laughing. "Maybe when things get a little more settled."

"How are you doing recovering from your accident?"

"I'm doing fine," he said, with a cheerful tone. "I've got a lot of experience dealing with injuries and with injured people," he pointed out, with a wry look outside at Jason in his wheelchair.

"I know, but you can't spend your whole life helping Jason and putting your own world on hold."

"It was hardly on hold. I went into the military and was gone for a big part of Jason's life," he corrected. "Now that I can't go back to that same line of work, it seems to be the perfect time to reconnect and to help him out."

"You've been helping steadily," she protested, "and he knows it."

"I hope so."

This conversation always made him feel guilty. He'd gone to serve his country, leaving Jason with their mother, which should have been fine, except their mother had gotten involved with a drink-loving ex-husband. Then Jason's accident had happened, while Cage was overseas. Things had gone downhill for his little brother ever since. Eventually their mother sobered up, so Cage signed up for another four-year tour. Later, both parents died in a car accident, about the same time Cage was in rehab, getting fitted for his first prosthetic. So it had been abundantly clear that it was time for Cage to come home permanently, not just on leaves here and there, and to reconnect fully with Jason.

Years ago Cage had been rather desperate to leave home and to have a life of his own, but, looking back, now he wished that he hadn't left Jason behind. Cage should have stayed and helped Jason get through some of the tougher parts of his life. However, it was what it was, and Jason was acclimating fine now.

"Thoughts?" Kat broke into his reverie.

Cage gave himself a headshake. "Ha, you know, just the usual what-ifs."

"Can't change them," she noted. "No matter how hard we try, we cannot change those."

"Would you ever really want to?"

"Sometimes, yes," she declared. "I'm a human. Just as you are. I've got things that I wish I could have done differently, yet I can't change it now. However, some things I can change. We can improve our situation, usually by helping other people."

He burst out laughing. "Well, if that's your pitch, convincing me to agree to help you, I already told you that I would." He could almost see her grin as she laughed.

"I'm just checking to confirm you're still really there for me."

"Absolutely I am, and, if I can do something, I would love to repay you for all you have done for us," he admitted sincerely. "I'm not sure about leaving Jason behind though."

"Ah, right, and I wasn't thinking about that," she conceded. "Maybe this isn't something you can do."

"Hey, now, … hang on a minute. That doesn't mean

Jason doesn't have a place to go for a few weeks because he does. Can I finish the job in that time frame? He's got a sports camp coming up."

"A sports camp?" she marveled.

"Yeah, he's sixteen, but he's hell on wheels when it comes to basketball."

"Literally hell on wheels," she teased.

"Exactly." And he knew that she understood.

"Barring unforeseen circumstances, you could be done in less than fourteen days."

"Good." Cage nodded. His brother had been in a wheelchair since … jeez what? When he was eight years old now? Cage shook his head, trying not to remember that point in time either.

"Well, I'm glad that he's doing so well. It makes being in that wheelchair a lot easier."

"Yeah, but we also know how desperate he is to get up walking again."

"Of course," she agreed. "I understand, from the notes I received from his doctor, that the surgery went really well."

"Yes, it did," Cage confirmed with a bright smile of relief, that went along with the conversation. "So, what's this call really all about?"

She sighed. "I have a missing K9," she began, "and one we want to reunite with a young boy, … if possible. I don't know if that's possible, but, at the very least, we want to confirm that the K9 is safe and in good hands."

"What does that mean exactly?" he asked, a little surprised to even hear about it. "I remember hearing something about you working with K9 dogs, but I didn't realize you were trying to set them up with homes. Is that a rescue thing?"

She chuckled. "That's the last thing I would think we are, but, in another way, it's morphed into that," she explained. "Let me explain."

She then went through an interesting but sad tale of a young boy who had spina bifida. "They applied for a dog for him, lucked out and got a War Dog that, although jumpy around loud noises, had a very gentle disposition. Apparently the boy and the dog took to each other, and it was such a wonderful bond for them, but sadly the parents were killed in a car accident, and the boy was put into the foster care system because nobody in the remaining family was willing or able to take him on. Meanwhile, the War Dog disappeared, and nobody really knows what happened to it."

Cage frowned, wondering how the dog just disappeared, especially if it'd been a family pet. But considering how panicked child services would have been when they showed up to tell a grieving boy about his parents who had died, on top of dealing with his change in circumstances, Cage could imagine it was tough all around.

Long after the phone call ended, Cage realized there was absolutely no way he could say no to helping out with this. He didn't even have a chance to respond to her request because she'd been called away. Yet Cage promised to think about it and to get back to her. As he looked out once more at Jason playing basketball on the court at the back of their family home, Cage realized it was wonderful timing.

He stepped outside, and, sensing his presence, Jason turned and waved.

He rolled over, sweat rolling off his face. "I can't wait for this camp, dude."

"Glad to hear it," Cage replied, staring down at his brother with a big smile. All that Jason had gone through had made him grow up fast. Yet he had always been a wise old soul, even from birth. He had to be the adult, when their mother was not so responsible. Cage sighed. "The only thing that bothers me is that I'll have to leave you all alone."

"Why? I'll be at camp, not exactly alone," Jason quipped.

"Yeah, but I won't be here at home. I'll be out of touch for a while. You can still call me though, should anything come up."

"Like what? Somebody running over me?" he teased, giving his brother a big goofy smile. Then Jason's tone turned serious, as he stared at his brother. "Not again." Jason nodded and added, "I'm a big boy now. I'm an adult, and I'm good with whatever life throws at me."

"I know you are," Cage agreed. "The young man I see today is a long cry from the boy I used to know."

"You're damn right," he declared, then eyed Cage curiously. "What will you do while I'm gone for a couple weeks?"

"Rest, relax, and hunt down a missing K9," he shared casually.

Jason nodded, then did a double-take. "What? What did you just say?" Cage laughed and told Jason about Kat's phone call. "Well, if Kat asked you to do it," Jason noted, staring at his brother hopefully, "you won't turn her down, will you?"

"I won't turn her down," Cage declared, with a smile. "She's done so much for us that it only makes sense to return the favor."

"Ha," Jason said. "You're looking forward to it, and it's got nothing to do with returning the favor, I'm sure," he suggested, as he rolled his eyes. "If you have the chance to go help somebody, you will."

"I will, yes," Cage confirmed, with a nod, "but it's also nice to know that you're doing well enough that I can leave."

"Absolutely you can." Jason gave a wave of his hand. "Go on. Get lost."

"Not yet. You leave for camp tomorrow though, right?"

"Yep, I'm all packed up and ready to go." He tossed a smile at his big brother. "As a matter of fact, I'm hungry. Do you want to order pizza for dinner? I'll go grab a shower and get changed, then double-check that I'm all ready to go."

"What time are you pulling out in the morning?"

"At six a.m.," Jason called back.

"Oh, that's early."

"Yeah, so you can be up and at it even faster than you thought," Jason pointed out, laughing. "I know the way your mind works. You were already figuring out how quickly you can pull out. By the way, where's this kid at?"

"He's not in town but local enough—Detroit."

"Oh, interesting." He turned to face Cage, mischief in his gaze. "Risa is there. You could run into her."

"Maybe, but I won't be talking to her."

"Do me a favor and say hi for me, if you do see her. She was always nice to me."

"She was always really nice to everybody," he admitted to Jason and shrugged. "That's got nothing to do with it."

"Actually it does. You know as well as I do that it has everything to do with it."

He shook his head. "No, it doesn't." He tried to make it sound as if he wasn't open for this discussion, but Jason just laughed at him.

"You can't hide forever."

"Sure I can," Cage muttered, as he watched his little

brother wheel himself into his bedroom, thinking to himself that it had worked so far, so why the hell wouldn't it work any longer?

And, with a headshake, Cage went to tell Kat that he was in, but, rather than calling her, he pulled out his phone and sent her a text. **I'm in. Send me the details you've got, and I'll confirm when I arrive in town. Jason leaves for camp at 6:00 a.m. tomorrow morning, so I'll head out shortly afterward**. He got a thumbs-up back from Kat, and moments later the file arrived.

He really loved that about Kat—how organized she was. She always seemed to be on top of everything. Even if you didn't think you needed or wanted it, she was right there getting it. You had to love that in somebody.

Whistling, he searched his Contacts and ordered pizza. It would be his and his brother's last night together for a few weeks, so they might as well make it a good one.

CHAPTER 2

C AGE REOPENED THE digital file on his phone, wondering if more information had been added to it since he last looked. How was anybody supposed to find anything when there was basically no information at all? When he'd complained about it to Kat, she'd laughed and explained how that had been one of the challenges she'd been facing ever since they started doing this. The files were mighty slim, but, so far, they'd had phenomenal luck.

"*Great*," Cage muttered to himself. That just put more pressure on him to do equally well. Not only would his pride not accept anything less, he knew his brother wouldn't accept anything less either. It's not that they were competitive, but they were competitive. All in good fun, of course, but it was a constant reminder that, if Cage wanted to do this, he would need to step it up.

No doubt that was a foolish attitude when it came to this stuff because who knew if the War Dog was even alive? The fact that nobody seemed to know where it could be was already extremely worrisome. They were great dogs, but they were accustomed to being well cared for. However, if not, then they could survive by hunting food on their own just fine. But then again, nobody wanted a War Dog out on its own, feeding itself as needed. It could take down other dogs, cats, small animals, even humans, if need be, but they weren't bred for that. It would go against their instincts, but, if starving, they would find a way to survive. So Cage hoped he didn't find anything to suggest that was happening.

It would break his heart if he located the dog, only to realize it had been euthanized because of its own actions, or because of ill health due to mistreatment or abandonment. Why did people expect a dog not to fend for itself? It was an animal first and foremost, and survival was the strongest instinct ever. It would be impossible for the dog to *not* look after itself, and that was an unfortunate scenario in many cases. Cage absolutely loved animals, so even contemplating this was hard.

After driving for ninety minutes or so, he now stood outside the small suburban house where the family had lived, when the parents were still alive. One of the things Cage always liked to do was walk around the scene of the crime, so to speak, and, in this case, it was the last scene of the boy's happiness. Cage wanted to confirm that nothing was out of place. He wandered around, surprised that the residence hadn't been sold.

After a few minutes, a neighbor came out and glared at him. "You looking for something?"

He nodded, put a pleasant smile on his face, and walked over to talk to the heavy-set woman who looked as if she had a grudge against everybody.

"I was hired," Cage began, "to come look for the missing dog that used to live here."

Her eyebrows shot up. "The War Dog?"

He nodded. "Yes. Did you have any problems with the dog?"

She shook her head. "No, I sure didn't, though some people around here might have, but he was perfect with

Brian," she shared somberly. "For that reason alone, I would forgive that dog anything," she murmured. "The boy had a tough go-round. I don't even know where he is now." She looked at him and asked curiously, "Do you?"

"Not yet. I haven't made contact with him, but I plan to. I'm pretty sure this situation must be a terrible struggle for him."

"Yep, it must be. He was very close to his family, and it was just him and his parents, so losing them left him high and dry, with nobody to look after him."

"I'm sorry to hear that," Cage muttered. "Everyone should have somebody."

"Yeah, they should, but, from what I can recall, Brian's mother had a much older sister, so I doubt she could take on the boy, particularly considering Brian's in a wheelchair. It's one thing to take care of a healthy child, but it's another to accept responsibility for a disabled one."

Cage nodded, knowing exactly how that felt. "My younger brother is disabled," he shared. "So I know exactly what you mean."

"What about you? Do you have anything to do with your brother?"

"Absolutely. We live together," he declared, with a smile. "He's at a basketball camp right now, while I'm out looking for this dog."

"Basketball camp?" she repeated.

He nodded. "My brother is sixteen, and we're very close. I was in the military, until a mission sidelined me," he stated. "I've got my own injuries to deal with now," he murmured. "My brother is doing great, but it wasn't always that way. I do remember all the pain he went through."

"Yeah, I don't think it can be an easy road in this

world," she muttered. "Brian's parents were basically good people, and nobody deserved to die like that. And I believe some suspicions were raised surrounding their deaths, which just makes it even worse."

He frowned at her. "I hadn't heard anything about that. Would you mind clarifying?"

She hesitated and shrugged. "I've got nothing to prove it, just what Fiona told me in confidence, but a lot of bad feelings existed between Oliver and his sister-in-law."

"The one who wouldn't take the boy when they died?"

Martha nodded. "Yeah, but she's too old. She might be close to my age. Besides, just because two people marry doesn't mean the rest of the family gets along."

"Understood." Cage nodded in understanding. "Although not everybody is geared for that kind of commitment—to take on someone else's child—and sometimes even family members aren't the best choices."

"Maybe, but that boy needed somebody to step up, and, when nobody did, he got shuffled off to a foster home," she muttered, "and that ain't a place for anybody, especially someone like him."

Cage didn't ask her why she didn't try to get him herself. He knew that, when people weren't family, it was hard for someone to navigate the fostering or adopting process, and the courts were quick to use the foster care system. "I'll be talking to Brian," Cage repeated, "and hopefully I can get a good idea of how he's doing."

"If there's any answer for him, any place for him that'll get him out of foster care, maybe you can help," she noted, and such sadness filled her expression. "God knows I tried. I talked to the cops and everything, but family came first, and—if there's no family, and if you can't prove you have the means to keep and to care for him—it didn't matter, so off Brian went."

"How did he take it?"

"He went kicking and screaming, as far as I could tell. I cried for days, but I'm on Social Security, and I don't have any way to make a living either," she muttered. She stared off in the distance. "Life is brutal if you're without money."

"Sometimes money is not as selective as we want to think," he offered. "My brother and I didn't come from money, but he's doing okay now. It was a hard road though, and for the longest time our mom was a single parent, and I know that was … Just the thought of having kids was enough to stop potential suitors, and finding out Jason was a disabled child, … that canceled almost all her dating life."

Martha smiled and nodded. "And maybe that was a good thing."

"Yeah, maybe it was," Cage agreed. "I don't have any way to know. I just know that, for the longest time, our lives were a little rough, but we had each other, and that's what counted. She remarried my father eventually, but we lost both of them a while back."

Martha eyed him approvingly. "When the chips are down, sometimes all you've got is each other. If you hear from Brian and if you get any chance to say hi for me, please do. He's a good kid, wise beyond his years. He's also quite the math whiz. He told me that he would grow up and be a mathematician—that is until he got the dog, and then he wanted to be a vet, so he could help protect dogs like that one."

"What did he call the dog?" Cage asked. "I have the military name for him in the files, but it's not necessarily the same as what the child might have called him."

"He called him Scotty after some guy in *Star Trek* or something," she replied. "Brian told me that his ears and rotund face looked just like him."

"Rotund face," he asked, with an eyebrow raised, "on a War Dog?"

She laughed. "I think it had something more to do with Brian dressing up the dog for Halloween."

"I can't imagine." Cage frowned at her. "I mean, I would love to see it, but I just can't imagine a War Dog dressed up in some costume."

"That's also why the two of them got along so perfectly. I know they were both heartbroken when the parents didn't come home that day," Martha added, "and now the house is just sitting here."

"Any idea who it belongs to?"

"I imagine the bank, or maybe it goes to the boy. For all I know, it's caught up in the courts, while some fake claim is made to take it from Brian."

"There will always be people like that," Cage muttered, then said goodbye. He smiled at her as he turned to walk away, wincing as his ankle joint caught ever-so-slightly.

"You've got a prosthetic yourself?" she asked.

"I do," he replied with a smile, turning back. "Plus, a few steel plates, a few things missing. That's just the way we come home from war these days."

She sobered and nodded. "Ain't that the truth? You take care of yourself now." Then she walked back into her house.

Cage headed to his car, and, taking one last look at the lonely empty house, he whispered, "You deserve another life too. Not just people need to be taken care of but also property, and everybody forgot that here. Someone should give a damn about the house that looked after that family while they lived here."

With one last glance around, Cage got into his vehicle, wondering where he should go next. Just as he was about to pull out, a familiar face walked by.

She stopped, took one look, and her eyebrows rose. Suddenly she shook her head, turned, and walked back in the opposite direction. Cage had no idea what seeing Risa again would be like, so he just got a first-hand experience with it.

He called out from his car window, "You didn't used to be afraid."

She stopped, then turned and glared at him. "I'm not afraid."

"Then why did you turn and walk away?"

"Maybe a better question is, why are you even here?"

"Not because of you," he stated, with half a smile, looking her over greedily. They hadn't left things on the best terms, as he'd wanted to go into the military, and she'd wanted nothing to do with it. But before all that, they had been best friends, first loves. They had been all those things that people smiled and wrote books about, but nobody ever seemed to write books about what happened when things didn't go well.

She walked back over, took one look, and asked, "So you're really home now, *huh*?"

"I am home, have been for a while," he replied. "How are you doing?"

She shrugged. "I'm fine." She frowned at him intently. "What about you?"

"I'm good. Why?"

She hesitated and then said, "I've seen Jason a time or two."

"Well, you could probably see him a lot more than that if you wanted to. He's always been very fond of you," he shared. "He told me to say hi if I saw you."

"He told me about your accident."

Cage nodded, his expression noncommittal. "Good," he noted. She deserved the truth, and he would have had a hard time telling her about that. "It's good that you know, so, when I stumble and fall, it won't be a surprise."

Immediately her face twisted in concern. "Does that happen?"

"Not so much now," he said, with a wave of his hand, "but it used to."

"Why is that?"

"Because I have a better prosthetic now," he stated, with half a smile.

"Are you using the same person that Jason is?"

Cage nodded. "That woman is hell on wheels for getting us back on our feet," he declared with a growing smile. "It's because of her that I'm here."

"What do you mean?" she asked, leaning in and studying his face. "You're seeing her?"

"Hell no, nothing like that. I'm here at her bequest. She's married and has what, two, maybe three kids? God only knows, it seems they multiply every time I'm there."

She snorted at that. "That's got to be tough. You didn't want kids. That much I remember all too well."

"Where the hell did you get the idea that I didn't want kids?"

She frowned at him. "You told me yourself, right before you left."

He couldn't remember saying any such thing and stared at her uncomfortably for a while, before he finally shrugged.

"I sure don't remember that, but whatever."

"What do you mean, … *whatever?*" she asked, narrowing her gaze, her temper starting to spike.

He grinned at that. "Still got your temper, I see."

She shook her head. "Oh no you don't," she countered. "I've only just seen you, and you're already egging me on."

"Not at all," he argued in all seriousness. "You look good, and I'm absolutely delighted to see you."

She stared at him in surprise, flushed now, and then nodded slightly. "Thank you. … It's nice to see you too."

He could see that she wanted to ask more questions, but he turned on the engine instead. "I do have to go, but it was great to see you again." With a smile, he returned his attention to the road, and, not giving her a chance to say any more, he pulled out and drove away.

RISA HARNEY STARED at the vehicle taking Cage away once again. It seemed as if, for all her life, all she'd done was watch him leave. He'd been a year ahead of her in school, and he'd left to go to university. Then he left her to go into the military, and, even now, once again he was driving away.

She knew it was stupid, fanciful even, but just once she wanted to be the one who drove away. In truth, she wanted to be the one who made him stay, instead of driving away. They'd once had a hell of a relationship, as steamy as they came, but it wasn't enough to keep him by her side. She wanted him to be free. She wanted him to go do whatever it was that he felt he needed to do, but she hadn't expected him to really go and do it without her in his life. She never wanted him to just leave her behind without another thought.

She'd thought for sure that he would find something nearby, something that would keep them together, but he hadn't. He had disappeared into the military machine, and she hadn't really seen him much since then.

It had been a fluke that she'd seen Jason at one of the recreation centers, when she was playing volleyball, and he was there with his ever-present basketball, and she'd had a chance to talk to him for a few minutes.

He told her a few things that she hadn't really understood about Cage, things that had made her stop and question why Cage had always been driven to enter the military and was always driven to a life of service. Now she realized it had mostly been because of Jason. She hadn't understood that Cage blamed himself for Jason's accident, and so Cage had been trying to make up for it ever since.

She hadn't really understood that Cage had always been one to assist anyone in need, not until she remembered all the times *before* Jason's accident—where Cage had volunteered to help people and had gone out of his way to do more than most people would, even those who were dedicated service types. In time, though it didn't come to her quickly, she realized that the military made sense to Cage. He'd served his country because he could, helped out because he could, and, in some way, it made him feel as if he was doing something because his brother couldn't.

And now, as she stared down the road, where Cage had disappeared from her view, she realized that he still had the same effect on her as always.

She hadn't exactly been welcoming. As soon as she'd seen him, she wanted to turn and walk away. It was almost as if she understood that fate was calling, and, whether she was ready or not, now fate was making her answer the call.

Shaking her head, she headed back to her car. Her girlfriend had moved into this neighborhood not all that long ago, but was now regretting her decision after some weird things had happened. So Risa had been staying with her off and on to make her feel better. Risa hadn't had or seen any weird incidents, but her girlfriend Celina was adamant that something bizarre was going on.

Risa tried to tell her that it was time to move if she was that uncomfortable, because Risa didn't want her friend to spend her whole life avoiding places because she thought it had a bad vibe, a comment guaranteed to get Celine's back up. And that is exactly what had happened. Celine got her back up and dug in her heels. Risa's friend had always had a worst-case-scenario mentality.

Risa threw her bag into the back of her car and headed home, and, just as she got there, her girlfriend buzzed her.

"Did you make it home okay?" Celine asked.

"I did," Risa muttered into the phone, as she grabbed her bag. "However, I can't keep doing this. You have to find another solution."

"Maybe. … I did meet my neighbor today."

The flirty tone and little-girl excitement in her voice made Risa groan. "Celine, that's probably not a good idea."

"Oh, come off it," she replied. "I mean, if I can't sleep alone because of the neighborhood, and I'm so uncomfortable being on my own, I might as well sleep *with* somebody."

"Sure, but maybe you should vet him a little first," Risa warned. "You do have a tendency to leap into relationships pretty quickly," she muttered.

"I know," Celine conceded, "and I can always count on you to keep me grounded."

"And yet you're ignoring me right now."

"Not at all," she declared. "I'm taking your advice under consideration, and then I'll ignore it." With a peal of laughter, Celine added, "Besides, he's lived here for a long time. He tells me that there's nothing to worry about in the neighborhood, but … I don't know," she muttered. "This place still seems to be a strange place to live."

"Which is why I keep telling you that it's time to move."

"I just got here though," she replied, "and I can't afford to lose my deposit."

"You only have to stay two months, first and last, because you didn't sign a lease."

"No, I didn't, thanks to you," she muttered, with a sigh. "It always seems as if you're looking out for me. And I appreciate that. I really do," she stated, with a laugh. "Anyway, I've got to run. I'm having lunch with my neighbor." With that, Celine quickly dashed off, before Risa could say anything more.

Staring down at the phone, Risa shook her head. "Good God," she muttered. Her friend really didn't like sleeping alone, but sleeping with just anybody wasn't the answer. Risa sighed, tossed her overnight bag on the counter, then quickly opened it up, adding these few items of laundry into the washing machine, and got it started. She put on the teakettle, while she crashed on the couch.

All she wanted to do was contemplate the return of somebody into her world that she hadn't really thought she would ever see again, or, if she did, it wouldn't be often. However, this was one of those strange circumstances that she wasn't very happy about. Yet she didn't have any reason to be unhappy. It was just a change, something she hadn't initiated. She had a feeling that the universe was laughing at her—and probably not for the first time.

Her mother called soon afterward. "What are you doing?" she asked in that parenting voice that urged Risa to *Tell me the truth or else.*

"I'm just sitting here, having a cup of tea."

"I tried to call you this morning," she stated in an accusing voice.

"Yes, and I was over at Celine's."

"Again? You can't just continue to sleep over there. If she doesn't feel safe in her own neighborhood, she really needs to move."

"I told her that," Risa pointed out, "but she's not too interested."

"Of course not. She's got you coming and going at all hours of the night, doesn't she?"

As usual, her mom went on a tirade about it for the next twenty minutes, then finally she slowed down. Now Risa had a chance to speak. "Did you have a reason for calling?"

"I was just checking to confirm all was well," she snapped, "only to find out you were being foolish with that friend of yours again. Celine is a big girl and needs to take responsibility for herself, rather than dragging you into her business."

"Well, I'm hardly being foolish," Risa muttered, "and nothing is different or changed around here."

"How come you sound different then? What's the matter? What happened?"

"Nothing happened," she snapped.

"Oh, now I know something's going on."

"Nothing's going on. I just saw somebody I wasn't expecting to see today."

At that, her mom stopped and then stated forcefully,

"*Cage.*"

Risa gasped. "Why would you even say that?"

"Because he's the only person I know who can rattle you," her mom declared in a triumphant voice. "Tell him to get lost. He's a loser."

"What the hell, Mom? That's not something you can say about anyone, much less a veteran. So why on earth would you say he is a loser?"

"Because he walked away from you, and you know that as well as I do."

"You also know that he had his reasons and that I told him to go."

"Sure, but where did he go when he came back? It's not as if he called you after that."

Risa winced at that.

"Or did he?" her mom snapped.

"Well, he might have, and I might not have picked up because I was a little pissed off. I was still really mad at him."

First came silence. Then her mother stated, "You really are great at sabotaging everything you want, aren't you?"

"*Gee, thanks, Mom,*" she muttered, with a sigh, "as if I need to hear this right now."

"Maybe not," she conceded, "but maybe you should look at why every time something good in your life happens, you intentionally screw it up, so it disappears." And, with that last barb, her mom said, "Drink your tea. It'll make you feel better." With those final words, she disconnected.

Risa stared at her cell, then tossed it on the couch beside her. "God, why do I even begin to tolerate you?"

Of course she was her mother, and it was just the two of them. Plus, her mother had always been this way, one day saying that what Risa did was smart, then the next day telling her how she was an idiot. It was almost as if her mother could easily be persuaded to take Risa's side, but, when she questioned Risa about her why, her mother shimmied back and forth like a bouncing ball. Her mother was an enigma that Risa found hard to understand. Her mother claimed to be checking to see which way Risa was leaning—and, if she would only make up her mind, the vacillation wouldn't be necessary on her mother's part.

Risa had laughed at that because it made absolutely no sense. To Risa, her mother's message was that Risa was always doing it wrong.

"Well, I'm just trying to get you to think, something you don't do that much. So I have to push you to really think about what you're doing and whether what you're doing is really what you want to be doing," she'd explained.

Talk about confusing. Her mother was nothing if not full of double-talk, making Risa question if her mother even knew what Risa was talking about in the first place. Yet, her mom was right on one thing though; tea did make her feel better.

As Risa sat here, she knew that Cage's family home wasn't that far away, yet far enough that it could be about a two-hour drive with traffic, just one way. He was on the outskirts of Lansing, and she was on the outskirts of Detroit, which she'd been hating for a very long time. It just wasn't the easiest place for her to love because her mother wasn't the easiest to deal with. Risa loved Lansing, but that's where Cage called home, so she'd left around the same time as her mother had moved here as well.

"Not moving there," Risa stated out loud. She dreaded even the thought of it. No way in hell she would subject herself to that torture of seeing more of Cage.

Her mom would just laugh and comment that Risa would grow up one day. Whatever that meant, Risa didn't want to know. The truth was, she still wasn't ready to go back there. However, she had been thinking about it lately. She just didn't have any reason one way or the other, and that was more troublesome than anything.

After her bath, she grabbed a bite to eat, then settled on her deck with another cup of tea and a book. As she sat here, she couldn't relax because she kept thinking about Cage.

Finally admitting it was a losing proposition, she called him at the same old number that he had had years ago. When he answered, she asked, "Why are you even in town?"

He snorted with laughter. "Wow, didn't take you long to reconnect."

"Maybe, then again, maybe I'm just looking for a way to disconnect permanently."

"Maybe so," he replied, "since obviously you were pissed the last time I was in town. You didn't even pick up when I called, then never called me back."

"No, I didn't, and I shouldn't be calling you now either."

"Probably not," he agreed, with a smile in his tone, "but you did. So what's it all about?"

"I want to know why you're in town." When he didn't give her an answer right away, she asked the question that was really on her mind, without even thinking it through. "Or are you here with someone?" Wincing at her immediate assumption that he was probably *not* alone, she waited. "In which case just tell me."

"Would it make any difference?" he asked curiously. "I mean, you made it clear that you didn't want anything to do with me the last time I was here."

"I was also very angry and upset, since you'd come home and hadn't told me."

"I was in the process of telling you. I left flowers for you in the lobby, but you wouldn't even give me a chance to say anything."

She frowned. "I don't remember any flowers."

"Of course not," he muttered. "You were too busy jumping down my throat. Somebody told you that I was in town, and, because I hadn't rushed over to see you first, … in your eyes I was guilty, and you were livid and pissed off. God only knows what I was guilty of, but it was enough to send you into a tailspin."

"I don't remember," she said. "All I knew was that you were home and that you didn't care enough to come see me."

"I cared enough," he countered, "but you made it very clear that I wasn't welcome. So I figured you had somebody else on the hook."

"On the hook," she repeated, almost laughing at the phrase. "God, I don't even know why I called you."

"Well, when you figure it out," he noted calmly, "call me back." And, with that, he disconnected.

She stared down at the phone, absolutely positive that her world had gone bananas. She shouldn't have called him in the first place, and no way they should have just had that crazy-ass conversation. But the fact of the matter was, she hadn't stopped caring for him, and, if he was here in town again, maybe there was a chance that they could clear the air and could see if they had any potential future together.

Then again, he hadn't told her if he was here visiting somebody or if someone else was in his life. She was still lost in thought when Celine called her back, bubbling over about her new boyfriend.

"Good God," Risa muttered, hearing the silly girl rave on and on. The last thing Risa wanted was to be like Celine, who went from one guy to the next, as if they were tissues or something. At the same time, something always seemed to be happening in Celine's world that made Celine happy, and a lot could be said for that. Though Risa didn't know what exactly, and right now she could do with any distraction at all.

When her girlfriend finally ran down of things to talk about, Risa asked, "What about being scared in your neighborhood there?"

"Oh, about that, he told me that one of his neighbors here was murdered."

"What do you mean, murdered?" Risa asked.

"Yeah, apparently a young boy and his parents lived here, but the parents were murdered, and the boy was put into foster care, so it just was very sad energy. You know how I've always been sensitive that way, so I'm pretty sure that's what I was picking up."

"Do you know what happened?"

"No, he didn't say a whole lot, just that the parents were killed in a car accident."

"How is that murder?"

"I don't know, but he said *murdered*, and I didn't question it. All I can tell you is what he told me, but it explains why I was feeling so bad. So I should be fine tonight."

"Fine tonight," Risa repeated, hearing a note in her girlfriend's tone that Risa wasn't sure she liked. "Did you bring him home?"

After a pause, Celine replied, "I'm going to make it an early night. So I'll talk to you tomorrow." And, with that, Celine disconnected.

Risa groaned, knowing exactly what her girlfriend had done. No matter how many warnings Risa gave her friend, Celine always ended up doing this. She jumped into relationships and into bed without even thinking it through. Celine kept telling Risa that she should try it herself more often, if for no other reason than to de-stress.

Maybe that was one way to de-stress, but Risa preferred to at least know the guy's last name before she jumped into bed with him. With a headshake, she turned out the lights. Only as she drifted off did she note that the empty house Cage and she had been standing by could have been the one that housed the family that had been murdered.

Instinctively Risa knew that was exactly why Cage was in town.

CHAPTER 3

RISA WOKE UP the next morning, pondering the empty house and the murder scenario that Celine had told her about the previous night. It was too early to call her girlfriend, particularly if she'd had somebody spend the night. When she called Cage, it was on instincts alone.

When he answered, he muttered, "That didn't take long."

"Does your presence have anything to do with the murder in that house?"

After a moment of silence, he asked in a brisk tone, "Who told you it was a murder?" She quickly explained about Celine. "I remember Celine," he noted in a dry tone. "Do you really trust anything that comes out of her mouth?"

Risa winced. "Maybe not, but it did happen to be the house where you were."

"Well, that was the area where I was," he clarified cautiously.

"Don't prevaricate," she muttered. "It's either the reason you're here or something similar."

"Well, it's something similar," he admitted. "The same little boy who lived in that house and lost both of his parents had a retired K9 War Dog," he explained. "That dog has gone missing since the parents were killed in the accident, and we know the dog isn't okay at the moment, since nobody knows where he is. So, I'm here to try and find him."

She stopped and stared down at her phone. "Are you serious?"

"Yes."

She gave a headshake. "I don't even know if I should believe you."

He half snorted into the phone. "Have you ever known me to lie?"

"No," she replied. "That's one thing about you. I would have said you're very honest."

"Would have said?" he asked sharply. "Do you really think I've changed?"

"No, maybe not." She didn't know what to say. "It all just seems so far-fetched."

"Maybe so, but then we have a little boy who's missing his dog, and we have a War Dog who already gave so much of his life in service for the American people. So it would be nice to think that he could at least have a few years of a nice and easy retirement."

"Was it retirement when he lived with the little boy?"

"Yes, apparently they bonded," Cage shared, "and, since you grew up with a dog that you absolutely adored, I'm sure you can understand."

She winced at the reminder. "I bawled for days and weeks when I lost Roscoe."

"I know," he agreed, "and anybody who has a love of animals would understand."

"Maybe," she muttered, "but my mom sure didn't." He started to say something and then stopped. She smiled. "You do have a little better control over that mouth of yours."

"No, I'm not so sure that I do, but your mother is an

exception all by herself."

"I know, and I've got to warn you that she hasn't gotten any easier."

"Why are you warning me?" he asked, with a note of humor. "It's not as if I'm likely to see her." She didn't say anything to that, until he broke in with a sharp tone, "Or am I?"

"I don't know, maybe not. I have no idea where you are and what you're up to. I'm certain she wouldn't be terribly welcoming regardless."

"Of course not," he replied. "I wasn't good enough for her little girl."

"Nobody's good enough for her little girl. Not even her little girl, apparently," Risa noted.

"Is she back to bashing you again?"

She winced as he picked up on that. "Well, you weren't around to bash, so I became the next best thing."

"God, she is such a bitch," he swore.

Risa smiled at that. Cage had always been a hell of a defender, and her mother had always respected the fact that she could never push Cage around.

Cage added, "I really should have a talk with that woman."

"Please don't," Risa said in alarm. "She wouldn't take it well."

"Maybe not," he agreed in low tones, "but, if one person needs a good telling off, it's her."

"You did tell me one time that you thought you were the right person for that job," she noted, "but she definitely hasn't gotten any easier to live with. She's very abrasive and always looking to criticize."

"Yeah, I can see that," he muttered. "She's not my favorite person."

"No, of course not." Risa laughed. "You refused to follow her rules and do it her way."

He laughed at that. "The military doesn't exactly breed that type of person."

"Why not?" she asked curiously.

"No room for insubordination," he stated. "Authority and chain of command are everything, and loyalty follows that. If you're given an order, you do it without hesitation."

"So, it doesn't matter what they say, you just follow through? That could also be a problem."

"It can be," he agreed. "Sometimes people do buck the system and create change, but a lot of times people can't be bothered. So they just follow through with whatever it is they're doing."

"You were never much of a follower," she pointed out.

"You don't know me that well anymore," he replied, his voice slightly rough. "I grew up a lot in the military."

"How many years?" she asked.

"Eight. I was there for eight."

"Amazing. Time goes by so fast, you don't even really realize it."

"Until you turn around and suddenly find yourself on the outside looking in at an entirely different world, one that's changed a great deal since you went into the service," he shared, with more of a pensive note in his voice.

She asked, "Do you regret it?"

"Going in? … No."

She winced. What had she been hoping for, that he would have regrets, would have hated leaving her behind? Of course he wouldn't have. It was very much who he was. He had absolutely been on fire to go. "Are you happy that you went in?" she asked.

"If I don't regret it, then of course I'm happy," he said, with a note of humor.

"Maybe," she muttered, "but sometimes not everybody understands how much their lives have changed, until they come out and then have a lot of regret over things they've missed."

"It has been an adjustment," he conceded, "but I'm working on it, and I would say I'm doing just fine."

"Of course you are," she said, rolling her eyes. He had always been like that. "I can't imagine you *not* being fine."

"Another criticism?" he asked in a sharp tone.

"No, not at all," she stated. "That's really not my style, and you've always stuck to your guns and believed in everything you did. I've always admired that about you."

He was silent on the other end for a moment. "How come you never told me that before?"

She gave a half laugh. "I don't know. … I never thought to, I guess, and even now it feels funny. We're strangers in the night now."

"I don't know that we could ever be strangers," he noted, "but, when you've spent a lot of time apart, I imagine this is a fairly common side effect."

"Maybe," she muttered, ignoring him, while chewing on the idea of side effects. "Why didn't we work out?"

"Because I needed to go into the navy, and you didn't like that." He hesitated before he added, "You didn't want to be tied down."

"I didn't even know what that was back then," she clarified. "It was more about letting you be free."

Again came that odd silence, and he replied, "I didn't ask to be free."

"No, maybe not, but I guess I felt as if you *needed* to be free," she muttered. When another awkward silence came, she gave herself a mental talking to. This was not going as she had imagined it would. "Look. I didn't mean to dredge up old history. I just wanted to know if the reason you were here had to do with the murder."

"Interesting you would even ask that of me," he said in amusement.

"If ever anybody would get into law enforcement when they came out, it would be you."

"I was considering it," he admitted, "but I can't say that I got that far."

"No, but you haven't exactly reached out yet either, have you? Aren't you still looking at options?"

"You could say that, yes. But, right now, I'm really only here because of the War Dog, and I do have Jason to go home to."

"Sure, but for how long? Jason seems to be doing pretty darn well fending for himself. I see him up here sometimes."

"Well, if you hadn't moved so far away, you could have seen him a lot more often."

"Same for him too," she pointed out, "though he comes up here all the time."

"Good," he replied, and again that same awkward silence fell over them.

After another uncomfortable moment, she continued. "Anyway, I've got to go." That being said, she quickly disconnected.

Risa sighed, noting their socially awkward moments on the phone, the likes of which were generally only between two people newly dating or maybe between acquaintances. She never experienced the long-distance version of their relationship, as they had just broken up and gone their separate ways. She didn't know how she felt about him anymore, except that, as soon as she'd seen him, she felt that same instinct, that same pull. She immediately wondered what he had been up to, where he had been, and why he hadn't called her.

It was the type of a thing that came with missed opportunities and lost chances. Of course he hadn't called her since that one attempt, and she hadn't called him. She hadn't reached out in any way. She also didn't know that he'd been in a serious accident, until Jason told her something about it. Yet it was just in a passing comment. She still didn't understand just how injured Cage had been and doubted he would even talk to her about it.

Realizing how foolish she'd made the ending of their relationship, but not knowing what else she could have done, she got up and put on the teakettle. When the phone rang, she was surprised to discover it was Cage again. "Hello?" she asked cautiously.

"Still trying to run away, *huh?*"

Her eyebrows shot up, and she snapped back, "Hardly."

"Felt like it," he replied, his tone way too smooth.

She felt her face flushing with heat. "That's not fair. It just feels really awkward."

"Yet it shouldn't be," he noted. "We spent an awful lot of time together."

"Sure, but that was many years ago."

"Yes, but it felt as if some of those years just disappeared the longer we talked." She half smiled at that. "Or do you not agree? If I'm barking up the wrong tree here, you should just tell me."

"I'm not exactly sure what tree you're barking up," she

began, then she hesitated for a moment. Her next words all came out in a rush. "You're right though. It did feel as if the years were falling away. I'm not sure that's particularly positive though."

He snorted. "You didn't used to be quite so cautious."

"Right, but, then again, I've been hanging around Celine too much, and, if anything, that has made me even more cautious."

He gave a bark of laughter. "Well, that's a good thing because that girl is nothing short of a menace."

"I haven't heard from her this morning either, which makes me nervous, considering that she planned to sleep with some new guy last night," she muttered.

"That lifestyle isn't likely to keep her safe."

"I know, and the only reason you saw me over there in the first place is because she'd been feeling very unsafe in that location."

"And why is that? I do need to do some more research on that property and the people who lived there. I talked to a neighbor, and she gave me some information. She misses the boy quite a bit, apparently."

"Apparently? What does that mean?"

"I don't necessarily believe everything I'm told the first time around."

"That's probably a good thing. I don't think Celine's had anything to do with any of the neighbors yet. She's not exactly the friendliest girl either."

"Seriously?" he asked.

"Okay, my bad. She is not friendly if you're a female. She's not one to hide her feelings either."

"Now that I understand," he muttered. "If anything, she's always been pretty standoffish with other women, hasn't she?"

"I guess, but we've been friends for a long time."

"You're probably the one and only girlfriend she lets in. I think she sees other women as competition."

"Which is pretty sad," Risa noted, "because I'm not competing for anybody. I'm just working my way through the plans that I set out."

"Are you a physiotherapist?"

"Yes. … I didn't think you would remember that."

"I've thought a lot about it," he admitted, with a laugh. "I mean, considering how many physiotherapists I've visited over these last few years, it seems as if they've been a constant in my world."

"Wow, that's because of the injury you had," she stated, "but I don't do that kind of physio."

"What kind of physio do you do?" he asked.

She laughed. "I'm a pelvic floor specialist."

He digested that for a moment and admitted, "I didn't even know there was such a thing."

"Well, there is." Risa was giggling now. "So, I won't be offended if you don't want to come and have a session with me." They both had a good chuckle over that, and she smiled, suddenly realizing just how much at ease they had become on the phone. "You're right. It does feel as if some of the years have fallen away."

"Well, if you're not doing anything, how about going for coffee?"

"Now?" she asked.

"Why not? It might be a good idea."

"It might be a good idea?" she repeated, feeling odd when hearing his lax tone. "That doesn't sound very posi-tive."

"No, but I didn't want to push, and … sometimes anything can be seen as too much."

"I'm not that bad," she protested. He didn't say anything, and she sighed. "Okay, fine, so maybe I am a little more on the cautious side than some other people."

"And that's a good thing," he stated. "I won't ever argue about your being cautious. I get it that staying safe is always paramount, and, besides, I think it'll be good for us."

She rather desperately wanted to ask why he thought it would be a good idea but then realized she was probably better off not even bringing it up. If she mentioned anything like that, it would make her sound as if she was being thick and deliberately trying not to understand. "Fine then, coffee it is. No promises and no strings attached."

He burst out laughing. "I didn't ask for any promises and definitely *no strings attached*. I didn't ask for anything."

"No, and in some ways that was always something about you that drove me crazy."

Sounding surprised, he asked, "What? What could I possibly have done to drive you crazy?"

"You were always just so agreeable," she replied hurriedly, "and I know that sounds strange, but it's as if … nothing ever upsets you."

"Lots of things upset me," he stated, "and injustice is one of the big ones. People who don't respect other people, people who hurt other people," he added, "that was what I wanted you to understand. It was one of the reasons I was out doing what I was doing."

"And here I thought it was because of Jason."

Silence came on the other end, and then in a tone that she wouldn't have expected from him, he shared, "You could be right. I've done a lot of thinking about the guilt I always carried around."

"I never understood that," she muttered. "I mean, why do you feel guilty? You didn't run him over."

"No, but my mother did, and she was a drunk. If I'd been home, looking after him, it never would have happened."

She winced at that. "I'm sorry. I didn't know."

"No, it isn't something any of us talked about," he said, "and now, with her gone, it's almost a sense of freedom for Jason. Maybe being tied to her was a hardship in its own way, you know?"

"I'm sure it was," she agreed. "Yet he is a very outgoing, happy-go-lucky kind of guy."

"Yeah, he is just that, but he's done a lot of work to get there," Cage replied warmly. "I'm really proud of him."

"You should be."

Changing the subject abruptly, he asked, "Same coffee shop?"

She winced. "I don't think it's even there anymore, and, besides, we're still here in Detroit."

"I know. I hate this big city stuff, but I'm here for a job. I can't wait to go back to Lansing."

"I'm surprised you're even here," she said.

"I'm here for the job, but why are you here?"

"To get away. I needed a change, and this gave me the best options."

"Well, that's honest at least."

"I try," she replied, with a smile. "I know to you it may not seem that way, but I really do try."

"I'm not against it either way," he murmured. "Do you want me to come by and pick you up, or is there a place close by you can walk to?"

She thought about it for a moment and then named a coffee shop just around the corner.

"Good enough," he said. "I'll be there in what, ten?"

"Better make it twenty." She looked into the nearby mirror. "I'm not even dressed yet."

He laughed. "I would tell you to come in your pajamas, but I'm pretty sure you wouldn't. So we'll make it twenty then, and thirty if you need it."

"I don't think I'll need it, but you never know." And, with that, she disconnected, a big smile on her face, and she ran to get dressed.

CAGE SLOWLY PUT down his phone, then got up and picked up his keys, while thinking about what to do with the information Risa had provided. Finally he picked up the phone and called Badger.

"Hey, got an update already?"

"Not really, more of a curiosity—or a question anyway."

"Well, we're good for those too. What's up?"

He explained what Risa had just brought up, about there being a murder. Badger was really quiet for a long moment, then he replied, "I'll make some further inquiries into this. So, in the meantime, you watch your back. If somebody is involved who may have had something to do with their deaths, you know how desperate people can be to keep it under wraps."

"I do know," he confirmed, with a note of humor. "I'm just wondering what you might have gotten me into."

"No clue. Do you want out?"

"No, I don't want out," he declared instantly.

"Well, that was fast. … So that's good."

"Yeah, it was fast all right," he agreed, with a chuckle, "because I don't generally walk away from my assignments."

"No, but nobody would judge you for it if you did," Badger noted. "It's not the kind of work you do anymore."

"No, but I've been wondering about going into law enforcement or something along that line. I just haven't really sorted out what I want to do."

"Well, if we can do anything to help you get started, wherever you decide to go, you just let us know. We have a pretty solid network of connections."

"I won't say no, but I just don't have a clue what I want to do yet."

"There's no rush either. First off, let's solve this War Dog problem, and maybe, in the meantime, some answers will come to you."

With that, Cage disconnected and continued on to the coffee shop. He pulled up and parked in the back, then headed to the corner table in the rear. In a way, he needed a few minutes to himself to sort through some of the information Risa had provided that could be helpful.

He expected Badger to get back to him pretty quickly, but, if Cage could dredge up anything on his own, that was all the better. As he sat here, he lost track of time. When the nearby chair was pulled back, and somebody sat down across from him, he blinked, looking up from his phone for a moment, then smiled, recognizing Risa. "Well, hello there," he said, in a tone that used to always make her laugh.

Her eyes widened, and she burst out laughing. "My God, I haven't heard that greeting in a very long time."

"Well, there's always a first, even again," he stated, with a big smile. "You're looking good. Did I get a chance to tell you that last night?"

She winced. "I still feel like an idiot for running away."

He shook his head. "No need. Sometimes we just react and don't really know what to do about it."

"That's probably all I did, just a blind reaction. It makes me feel foolish, but I'm willing to get past it if you are."

"Absolutely." He smiled. "Shall we order some coffee?" She nodded, and, as she started to get up, he shook his head. "I'll grab it."

He checked on what she wanted and then proceeded to the counter to put in their order in. When he got back, she looked at him and noted, "You ended up with a bit of a limp, *huh*?"

He nodded casually. "Yeah. It goes with the territory, I guess."

"I'm not sure I want to know what happened," she muttered. "It sounds painful."

"Waking up afterward was a bit of a shock, and it took a while to get through it, but it's not as if I'm the first person to come home with this kind of injury."

"Unfortunately it seems all too common these days," she replied, studying him carefully, "but you appear to have adapted."

"As everyone does," he noted, with a gentle smile, "I have good days and bad days." It was obvious that she was contemplating that when he shrugged and added, "Mostly good days though."

"But not always?"

"No, not always. I won't lie."

"Of course not. That's not your style."

He grinned at her. "Nope, definitely not, as you should know."

"Sometimes I'm not even sure what I know anymore."

When the coffee arrived, he smiled over at her, lifted his cup, and said, "Cheers."

She grinned. "Seems it's been a long time since we had anything to say *cheers* about, hasn't it?"

"Sometimes we just have to make it what we want to make it," he murmured. "A lot of things in life we don't necessarily like, but it's not all bad."

"I'm glad you think so." She smiled at him. "So, about this murder …"

He looked at her and chuckled. "I figured you wouldn't let that go."

"Not if it's about a boy and his dog," she muttered. "That's all I've been thinking about ever since you mentioned it."

He nodded. "I have to admit it's the reason I jumped at it. It's hard enough for a child to lose his parents like that, but to also lose his dog? That doesn't seem fair at all."

"No, but it's also not fair for the foster family to be expected to take care of the boy and the dog. Not everyone is cut out for that."

"Maybe, but it sure would be nice if there was a way to make it happen."

"Do you think there is?"

"I don't know the answer to that question. There are so many unknowns, and I still don't know much about the case." She didn't say a whole lot, but he knew that it was percolating in her brain. He smiled. "Still looking out for the underdog, aren't you?"

"Is the little boy an underdog?" she asked, with a glance in his direction. "Or just somebody in need? Sob stories have always gotten to me."

"Agreed. I remember you crying at movies and generally having a hard time with anybody being hurt."

She murmured, "I just think that's part of being human and how some people are softer hearted than others."

Not a whole lot he could disagree with that, and he really had no intention to. She'd always been full of heart and a bit of a softie. Who could argue against that? He'd become a little more jaded and toughened up after seeing the state of the world around him, but that was his problem, not hers. "You should stay just the way you are," he said suddenly. She looked at him in surprise, and he shrugged. "You've always had a unique outlook on life."

"Ah, you mean, I'm naïve?"

"I don't know that I would call it naïve, but I think you had a certain innocence. It's definitely something special in this crazy world, and I think we all need more of it."

She stared at him, but he could tell that a pleased expression was on her face, and she shrugged self-consciously. He smiled. "Honestly, you're one of the good people in life," he shared, "and it would be really nice if we could keep that sense of childlike wonder in everything."

"I lost a lot of that."

"Growing up does that," he noted, with a smile. "It's been a lot of years."

"It has," she murmured. She gave a sudden headshake and suggested, "We need to talk about something a whole lot less depressing." She looked over at him and asked, "So, what is it that you're doing with this dog, and what is your plan for trying to find it?"

He smiled at her and then chuckled. "Of course it's all about the dog."

"It's definitely about the dog … and the little boy," she

stated abruptly. "The whole thing is a tearjerker, if you ask me."

He nodded. "Well, I don't have a whole lot of information yet. I've told my boss what you mentioned about a murder, and he's looking into it. He has a lot of connections in the military and in agencies all over, and we'll see what they come up with. In the meantime, I'm making an appointment to go see the little boy. I want to talk to him and see if he has any details, and I'll talk to the foster family. Naturally I'll have to talk to Child Services," he noted, "and hopefully, somewhere along the line, something will pop up to help me solve this mystery."

"It would be nice if it fell into place like that," she said. "It's depressing to think that he lost everything."

"A lot of us lose everything," he shared, "but that doesn't mean it has to be lost forever."

"No, but you and I both know that nobody'll give the boy his dog back."

"Maybe not, but that doesn't mean the military is prepared to walk away from the dog," he pointed out.

She shook her head at that. "As much as I want to believe that the military cares, you know it's much harder for me to wrap my head around it."

He nodded. "I know, and that's okay too," he said. "Not everything in life is so cut-and-dried or the way we want to see it. There are always other things that we don't know about, and, until we have all the information, there's really no point in stewing over it."

"Maybe," she conceded. "I can't believe how much the story of the dog upsets me though."

"I'll let you know what I can when I find out something," he offered. "It's not that I'm doing any classified work, but it is definitely not my story to share. I'll have to ask my bosses how that works."

She frowned at him. "Right, I hadn't even considered that angle."

"Don't worry about it." He laughed. "I didn't either, and it's on me to figure it out."

She nodded. "It's all so interesting to think about though. What happens to all of these lost War Dogs?"

"Well, in some cases, good things, and some other cases are not so good."

"I've heard some terrible stories about what they did with them after the Vietnam War."

His cheeks sucked in with the pain of that story too. "I know. I've heard the stories, but I choose not to focus on that now. I'm just glad we've learned from our mistakes, at least to some degree."

"Sometimes it's got to be hard not to focus on all that could go wrong," she muttered. "I mean, to think that even more could go wrong is just heartbreaking."

He nodded. "It is, and I agree. So we're focusing on the good stuff and going from there."

She smiled. "I forgot about that optimism you always had."

"It wasn't really even optimism," he clarified. "I think it was an understanding, an acceptance of the reality that I can only change what I can and have to try to find peace with the rest of it."

"That sounds like the old you."

"I am the old me," he confirmed. "Some things have changed, but not an awful lot."

"So why didn't you try to contact me again?"

He looked at her, then asked in a clipped tone, "Why

didn't you answer your phone the first time I contacted you?"

"Because I wasn't sure what to say," she admitted. "Just the same as when I saw you yesterday, … and I ran."

"Yeah, I'm still pondering that reaction myself," he said, with a look at her. "I can understand the sudden surprise and being uneasy maybe, or not sure what to say, but the running part? I just don't get it."

"It's very me, or have you forgotten that too? Surely not when you accused me of running away *again*. Whenever I get to a place in life that's uncomfortable," she explained, "I just walk away because I don't know what else to do."

"Are you still doing that?"

She winced. "Well, considering I took one look at you and ran, I guess so." He just nodded. "Why do you think I ran?"

"Well, the obvious answer is because you didn't want to see me," he replied.

She winced. "Yeah, that's the obvious answer, but it's not the real answer."

"Good. Did you already know that I had an injury and didn't want anything to do with me because of it?"

"God, no," she exclaimed, as she stared at him. "That had nothing to do with it."

"But did it though?" he asked, staring at her intently. "I do have a prosthetic. I just don't make a big deal out of it."

"Sure, but, for somebody like me who's in physiotherapy, that is not an issue." She frowned, "And your injury isn't obvious."

Her tone was just firm enough that he wanted to believe her, but he still remembered her taking one look and running. He just nodded to put her at ease. When his phone rang, he looked down at it and raised a hand. "Hang on. I've got to take this." Then he answered, "Hey, Badger. What's up?"

"Well, I have a little bit of information but not a whole lot and not a lot of it good."

"Okay. What does that mean?"

"It means that there is a chance she's correct. The police have kept an open file. They don't have any answers, so until something else develops, … it's definitely an open case."

"Yet murder by car accident?"

Risa immediately straightened, and her eyes went wide open.

Badger added on the sly, "I was asked to keep you out of their way because they are actively pursuing an investigation."

"Well, that's nice," he stated bluntly. "So am I."

Badger laughed. "I know, and I told him that. He wasn't terribly impressed, and they won't allow any interference."

"I highly doubt that anything I'm looking at will affect them."

"I did explain that we were on the hunt for a War Dog, not a murderer," Badger shared, with humor threading through his tone, "but he's aware that my men have a tendency to trip over things and to get in the way more than he would like."

"That's interesting," Cage noted, with half a laugh. "It's almost as if he knows you."

"Right? He didn't seem terribly friendly."

"Is it a problem?" Cage asked.

"No, it isn't. I know his buddy pretty well, and I'm sure I'll be getting a phone call from him very soon," Badger noted. "I expect they'll say that you can carry on as you are, and, should the investigations dovetail in some way, they very much want to be kept in the loop."

"Of course." Cage glanced over at Risa, who was listening intently.

"Other than that," Badger said, "watch your back." And, with that, Badger disconnected.

Cage pocketed his phone and looked over at her. "So, apparently the case remains open, and it is possible that the family was murdered," he shared in a low tone of voice.

She gasped. "Good God, is it even safe over there for Celine?"

"It's hard to say with the limited information we have," he replied, with a shrug. "But, unless she has done something to piss people off," he added, with a roll of his eyes, "then I'm sure she's safe."

"Yeah, I don't know about the *pissing people off* part," Risa acknowledged, "since she does have a tendency to be a little blunt when she's not happy."

"Ya think? If I remember correctly, that girl gets into trouble without too much effort."

Risa nodded. "I can't say that she doesn't because you know she can be a handful."

"Sometimes," Cage agreed, with a smile.

She winced. "Okay, so she tends to walk to her own drumbeat, but that doesn't make her bad. Still, I'll just send her a quick text and see if I get a reply. After all, she's with her *new man*, and I haven't heard from her today."

At the defensive tone in her voice, he smiled. "Believe me that I'm not saying she's bad by any means. I'm just not sure about this scenario I suddenly find myself in, much less her own scenario."

"That's the thing I don't understand either," Risa noted.

"What are you supposed to do about it?"

"Keep an eye out for any murder clues, while I keep searching for the dog. Then, if I find anything that pertains to the murder investigation, I will let the police know."

Her eyes widened at that. "Are you going to investigate this?"

"This?" he asked, looking at her curiously. "What is *this?*"

She frowned and shrugged. "I guess I don't really know. What is this?"

"I'm looking for a War Dog," he stated. "That is what I am here for."

"Right." She frowned. "It just seems so strange that the dog would be the priority."

"Well, it is in my case. That's what I came for."

"Right." At that, her tone turned a little more formal.

He studied her across the table and asked, "Now what's got you upset?"

"Nothing," she declared, her tone crisp, "absolutely nothing."

He rolled his eyes. "I didn't even know you would be here."

"No, of course not," she replied, her shoulders sagging. "You didn't, and it's not as if we've had anything to do with each other over the last eight years."

"Yet you think I've done something wrong?"

She looked over at him and winced. "How could you have?" she asked, with a small smile. "I'm just being foolish, with old resentments coming back."

"Well, maybe you should tell me what those old resentments are, so I can deal with them."

"I'm not sure I can," she said. "I didn't realize just how

much they were festering until you spoke up just now."

He nodded. "I think that's the trouble I'm having. I'm hearing the resentment, but I don't know what I did wrong. As I recall, you sent me off to war quite happily. You didn't want to be here dealing with somebody who would be coming back and forth, and you, … you wanted to be free."

"Free?" she repeated in fascination. "I wanted *you* to be free to go be you."

"And I did just that," he stated, looking at her puzzled, "and, when I came back into town a couple times, I couldn't get a hold of you. I even left messages."

"No, you didn't. I never got any messages." She stared at him. "Left message with whom?"

He looked at her, opened his mouth, slowly closed it, and then answered, "Your mother."

She sank back and pinched the bridge of her nose. "Good God. … You do realize I never got any of those messages, right?"

"I'm just now starting to realize that," he replied, staring at her. "Would she really have done that?"

"I wouldn't have thought so, but my mother is certainly capable of doing things we don't expect," she noted, "so my guess is she absolutely did." She shook her head as she stared around the restaurant. "Now I feel very strange." She looked back at him. "How many times did you leave messages?"

He shrugged. "The first three times I got a chance to call you. The first time I was just …" He gave her a half smile. "I was lonely. I was out in the middle of nowhere and wanted to hear your voice. I called, and you didn't answer, but your mother did. She told me how you were out enjoying your freedom. I asked her to tell you that I called and that I would try again. As it was, I had leave coming up, only you never answered my message. I tried calling you when I got back, and you didn't answer then either." He shrugged. "I left another message, but, after the third time, I figured you didn't want to hear from me anymore. So I stopped calling. I thought if you weren't trying to get back to me, the meaning was pretty clear."

"But I didn't get back to you because I didn't even know you'd called in the first place. Goddammit." She stared out across the room. "I didn't know. I swear to God, I didn't know. Then I was angry because you didn't call, so by then I didn't answer when you tried again."

He nodded slowly. "It occurred to me that it might be something like that, but I didn't have any reason to suspect that she would deliberately try to sabotage our relationship. I hadn't thought I was on the hit list, but apparently I didn't really understand." Risa just stared at him, and he could see the pain in her expression. "It doesn't really matter, you know? It's okay."

"What do you mean, it doesn't matter? All that time you thought I didn't care. And I thought you didn't care as well."

He pinched his lips together and then nodded slowly. "Well, that's the way it looked, yes," he acknowledged. "What was I supposed to think?"

"Of course that's what you would have thought," she grumbled, her bottom lip trembling. She pressed her lips together, and he realized she was close to crying. "When in truth I thought you didn't care."

"I didn't bring it up to make you feel bad."

She broke into a half laugh, half cry. "How can I not feel bad?" she asked. "I meant it when I told you to go off and to do *you*. I meant that sincerely because I really wanted you to be happy and doing what you wanted to do. It just never occurred to me that I wouldn't hear from you again. That you wanted to be alone or at least not with me." she explained. "Now to think that all that time I thought you had ignored me, you were expecting me to contact you, or at least to acknowledge that you had been in contact with me. It's just …" She shook her head. "It's just heartbreaking," she whispered.

"Well, at least you know now," he said.

She stared at him. "That doesn't help."

His lips quirked. "No, I can see that maybe it wouldn't help, but I can't see that it would hurt."

The waitress came back around then to offer to fill up their coffees. Risa accepted it, numbly holding out her cup to be refilled. When Cage shook his head, the waitress left.

Cage watched Risa carefully, not at all sure it was safe to just let her be right now. "I really didn't tell you about that to upset you."

"Right, and that's another thing, that if I gave it a chance, would it piss me right off, because how could you not be mad at me all these years? How could you not be disgusted, thinking I hadn't even tried to get back to you?" She frowned. "I mean, that was the last thing I ever would have done to you."

"I know," Cage agreed. "That's why I took it as being over and that you didn't want anything to do with me and that giving me my freedom was basically you taking your own freedom in stride."

She just stared at him numbly and pinched her lips closed together yet again.

"Hey"—he grasped her hand—"I'm sorry."

"No," she muttered, the tears clouding her eyes. "I'm sorry. It's not what …" The words couldn't come out, and she stared off into the distance, blinking rapidly to hold back her tears.

He gave her hand another gentle squeeze. "On the other hand, I'm no longer in the military, and I'm here. If nothing else, seeing me should totally piss off your mother."

She looked at him, and then a strangled laugh burst out. "Only you would see that as a positive right now," she muttered. "To even think she did that and knowingly set it up like that for me …"

"Is absolutely freeing," he declared. She eyed him in surprise. "It's freeing because it allows you to know who she is, what she is, and what she's prepared to do. She is prepared to … I don't know. She seems prepared to intentionally stop you from being happy."

"I don't disagree," she muttered, frowning at him, "but why? I'm her daughter. Aren't we supposed to want to see our children happy?"

"Yes, but does your mother strike you as the kind of person who is like everybody else?"

"No, you're right. She's definitely not the mother who is ever concerned about anybody other than herself, but good God," she muttered, squeezing his hand. "How could she do that? Why would she hurt you, who were out there in service to our country?"

"I don't think the fact that I was in the service made a bit of difference to her at all," he stated, with a note of amusement. "I think it was all about control, or maybe keeping you under her thumb, or maybe she really didn't think the relationship was good for you. So she was happy to do whatever she could to confirm it didn't continue."

Risa just stared at him and muttered, "You are way more generous than I am."

"When you've had a chance to think about it," he suggested, "chances are you'll understand where she was coming from."

"I will never understand," she bit off.

He winced. "I didn't tell you to cause a fight between you and your mother."

"No, that may not have been your intent," she noted, with a look in his direction, "but that's exactly what you've done." He groaned. Seeing him react, she shook her head. "It's not your fault."

"You do realize that, in this instance, I am absolutely going to get blamed."

She nodded. "For this, you probably will," she agreed, "but, for anything else, that's all on my mother, and that is something I cannot let her get away with."

"What will you do?" he asked, staring at her. "It's just the two of you. Maybe she did it to keep you close. You don't know her reasons."

"No, I don't," she replied. "It's possible you're wrong, but you and I both know, … chances are that's exactly what it was."

"But you don't know that."

"No, I don't." She shook her head again. "I'm just sitting here still dumbstruck over the whole thing, and it's not something I'll wrap my head around anytime soon."

"How has your relationship with her been going?"

She stared at him, then shrugged. "Not great. She's still very abrasive, still very critical. Even today she told me that you were a loser when I told her that I had seen you."

"Oh, wow, that's nice to know," he replied, trying for a note of humor and realizing he had failed when she shot him a look.

"She had no business saying anything after what she's done," she snapped.

Knowing it was probably best to just stay quiet, he tried to stay out of it.

Finally Risa groaned. "And here I am, snapping at you, and it's not your doing, or your problem."

"Sometimes we can't do anything about our families," he shared. "You know as well as I do that my mother wasn't the easiest either. Only after she ran over my brother and ruined his life did she quit drinking for a time, but it wasn't in time to make Jason's life any better. There was no way of saving him all that pain," Cage shared, "and, yes, at least she finally did smarten up with the time she had left. She did all she could for him at first, but that didn't change what happened."

"No," she muttered. "God, that is awful to even contemplate. I knew about that accident, but damn. … I'd forgotten the details."

"Probably just as well," he said. "It's not something that Jason or I want to dwell on because there's no joy in that."

She smiled. "And the two of you have always managed to let bygones be bygones."

"I think I hated her more than he did, even before the accident," Cage shared. "It's one of the reasons I went into the military because my attitude toward her was something I was really struggling with. When she and our father tried to make their relationship work again, I thought she might settle down. Yet all that happened was she started drinking again with our father.

"He promised me that he would get sober, and so would she. He also thought that, if I went into the service, it would be one less responsibility for them to handle. Still, it was

Jason who persuaded me to go. He said I wasn't helping and was actually hurting the issue, so I needed to find a way to control my temper and to let my anger go. I needed to find some space, some time, and some distance from all of it.

"Yet here Jason was, the wise old soul at eight years old. Leaving made me angry and made me feel guilty in so many ways, and yet I felt it was the best thing I could do to save our family. But leaving Jason?" Cage shook his head. "That was hard. And then when the accident happened? That was worse. If I had been in town, I'm not sure I could have contained myself. There I was, overseas, signed up for a four-year tour and couldn't go back on my word. So I spent every leave with Jason."

"I am so sorry," she whispered. She glanced around and added, "I need to go talk to my mother." He stared at her in horror. She smiled. "It's okay. It's not about you."

"Of course it's about me," he countered. "Man, if that woman finds out you talked to me …"

"That's probably why she spoke that way this morning," Risa shared. "She knows what's coming. Anyway, I can't stay here and hide. I'll face this and have a little talk with my mother about interfering in my life. What will you do today?"

"I'll go talk to the little boy, and then to someone handling his case at Child Services to see what other information I can dredge up." He hesitated, smiled at her, and asked, "You want to have dinner with me later?"

"Absolutely. I would love to have dinner," she confirmed, studying him. "You should hate me for everything that's happened."

He shook his head. "You're forgetting who you're talking to. I don't hate easily. If I did, I probably would have done something to my own mother."

She winced and then nodded. "That is a very valid point. Dinner it is. What time?"

"Seven," he said, as he stood up. "If you need to cancel, give me a shout." And, with that, he turned and headed to his car.

CHAPTER 4

RISA WAS VIBRATING with rage by the time she pulled up to her mother's house. Her mother had done well for herself. Surely because of the multiple husbands she had managed to snare and release, while keeping half of their assets each time. Risa stared up at her mother's latest house, one that her mother fully planned on keeping but was now caught up in some litigation over the residence with her ex.

Oddly enough Risa had liked most of the men her mother had brought home. But one of the things she had never quite understood was why they all liked her mother. They should have been able to see through her, but they didn't.

As Risa stormed up the front steps, the door locked right in front of her. She stared in disbelief. "Do you think that'll stop me from coming inside?" Risa asked in a low tone.

"Sure, it will," her mother declared. "You think I didn't see you coming out of that vehicle in a rage? You think I'll deal with that? Hell no. Take a hike, or I'll call the cops."

"You'll call the cops on me?" Risa asked in disbelief.

"Yes. I refuse to deal with that temper of yours."

"I don't have a temper. You're the one with the temper."

"Well, it looks to me that right now you're in a temper," her mother stated, "and I will not talk to you, not like this. So go away, and you should know that I have my finger on

9-1-1 right now."

Completely nonplussed, she stared at the peephole toward her mother. "So, you'll get the locks changed at the same time?"

Silence came from the other side of the door. "Crap, I forgot you had a key."

"Yeah, I've got a key all right, so go ahead. … Let's bring the cops into this. I'm sure they would love to know all about the lies you told Cage while he was out of the country, fighting for us all, you included."

"Oh God, is this about him?" she screeched, with a snort. "Grow up. He wouldn't bring you anything but trouble."

"And how would you know?"

"It's not as if he had any money. He had nothing to bring to the table. He was just another broke boy, and those are a dime a dozen."

"Really?" Risa pinched the bridge of her nose. "I know that's how you treat the men in your world, but it's not how I treat the men in mine."

"Yes, it is." She laughed loudly at that statement. "You just don't admit it, which makes you the fool. I at least own who and what I am," she declared. "You, on the other hand, just like to imagine you're somebody special. Wake up, girl. You're not special. You've never been special, and you'll never be special."

Risa's jaw dropped as she listened to her mother. Most of the time her mother was at least halfway reasonable, but right now she was on a tirade that didn't bode well for anybody. "I find it very odd that you would even talk to me that way," Risa pointed out.

"Because you're being a fool, and I have no time for

fools. If you've got something to say, say it, and it damn-well better be nice. Otherwise I'll kick you out of the family and disown you."

"Disown me from what? As I understand it, you must be low on money, so you're going back to court right now because you've lied and cheated your way out of another relationship. What the hell will you disown me for?"

"God, you're so naïve. That's not how the world works. You have yet to learn the game."

"That's funny because you didn't tell me how the world works. According to you, I've just been watching it from the sidelines, trying to figure it out."

"Well, you didn't figure it out, did you?" she snapped. "You're still sitting there, playing the whining little bitch." In exasperation, her mother opened the door and let her in. "If you weren't such a stick in the mud, you would realize that everything I've done, I've done for you."

"That's a load of BS," Risa declared, as she frowned at her mom.

Her mother rolled her eyes. "Good God, Risa, I don't see how I possibly could have raised such a naïve little girl."

"It's not that I'm naïve," she corrected. "I'm nice."

"Same diff," her mother snapped, glaring at her, "and don't you dare say I'm not nice."

She frowned at her. "Do you really think you're a nice person?"

"Of course I am, and I treat my men very well. I don't need you to tell me what I am and what I do."

"Oh, you treat them well for a little while, before you divorce them, take everything they have from them and from their families."

"Oh, *pftt*," her mother argued, making an odd sound.

"Don't even begin to think that way. These men know exactly what they're getting into, and it's a bargain. We talk about it ahead of time, and it's good while it's good. Then one day it's not good anymore. That's the problem with relationships. They're only good for a little while, and then they're not good anymore. I don't intend to end up without any money or anything to show for all the husbands I've put up with."

"Husbands *you* have put up with?" Risa asked, staring at her.

"God, now you sound like an imbecile, repeating everything I say," she snapped. "Just forget about it. It is absolutely none of your business."

That was true in a sense, but something splintered inside her. "So, it was none of my business that Cage attempted to contact me multiple times while he was away, and you didn't bother letting me know?"

"God, no, I told you before. The man is a loser."

"Yet you never said anything to him when he was here."

"Of course not," she spat. "You were dating him. What would I say? *Get lost?* I should have. That would have made a whole lot more sense than watching you mope around after he left."

"Yeah, part of the moping around was because I thought he didn't care."

"That is the truth. He didn't care," her mother declared, with a wave of her hand. "Surely you don't believe any of his crap. I knew he wouldn't stick around for long. If he hadn't left, I would have said something. No way would I let such a loser get his hands on you."

Risa wasn't even sure what she was hearing from her mother right now. "I am absolutely stunned."

"If you're stunned, it's your own fault," her mother snapped. "I've always been this way."

Her tone was so cross, probably because her daughter was questioning her. "Good God," Risa muttered. "There's absolutely no point in even talking to you."

"No, and if that's what you came to talk to me about, you can just get lost. I have no intention of apologizing or anything of that nature. He wasn't good for you, and I definitely didn't pass on the messages. Did you expect me to hide that? If I thought he would be any good for you, I would have been all over him."

Risa winced. "*You* would have been all over him? For yourself?"

"Well, I would have considered it, damn right. A girl's got to do what a girl's got to do, and there's nothing wrong with having a nice healthy stud in the bedroom. Lord knows I need it more than you do."

"Oh God," Risa muttered.

Her mother laughed. "I don't need your drama right now. If I'd only known I would end up with a prude for a daughter, maybe I could have fixed you early on."

"Looks as if we're both doomed to be disappointed," Risa declared, staring at her mother. She turned and walked to the front door. "I think I need to go away and just think for a while."

"Yeah or just go get laid. That will do great things for your psyche."

"You think so?" she asked. "Somehow the thought of ending up like you stops me from going there."

"That's just foolish," she said, with a chuckle. "If you think I'll leave you any money to blow, you're wrong. I fully intend to spend every penny I've got."

"You do that," Risa agreed. "It's not as if you've ever been very generous with your money up until now anyway."

"No, but my husbands have been there for you, haven't they?"

"Have they?" Risa asked, turning to face her.

She snorted. "It's not as if you needed it anyway."

Almost defeated at a world that Risa suddenly didn't recognize, she slowly headed back out to her car. As she got out to where she was parked, she stood and stared back at her mother's place for a long moment.

How was it even possible that they were related?

She knew her mother was probably wondering the exact same thing right now, and God knows Risa didn't have any answers for her. They were as opposite as chalk and cheese.

She opened up the driver's side door, and, as she went to step in, a man hollered at her. She turned to see her ex-stepfather, the latest one in a long line of stepfathers, walking toward her. She smiled at him. "Hey, Graham. How are you doing?"

"I'm doing pretty well. How are you? Every time I ask your mother about you, she doesn't tell me anything."

"No, we've just determined that it would be best to stay to ourselves at the moment," she muttered, staring back at the house, where her mom was even now peering out the window. "Are you still talking to her?"

He shrugged. "Well, my lawyers are, and every time I try to find out anything, she's not exactly supportive."

"Of course not. I'm pretty sure she's only out to get everything she can."

He winced. "I loved her, you know?"

She smiled at him. "That's what you're supposed to do. You're supposed to go into a marriage with love," she declared. "I'm not sure either one of us understands who my mother really is."

"It was that kind of a talk today between you two, *huh*?" he asked, looking at Risa worriedly. "Are you okay?"

"Yeah," she muttered. "Once again I've realized I don't understand who she is, and, even the things I thought I knew, I didn't know at all."

"Well, give her a bit of a break," Graham suggested. "She's never been very secure with money."

"That's for sure, though I've never really had anything to do with any money that came into the house," she shared. "I've always made my own way, and I don't know if that was her doing or not, but I guess I owe her for that."

"When you say that you've always made your own way"—Graham paused to look at her—"does that mean you didn't get the money I set aside for you?"

Risa frowned at him in astonishment. "I don't even know what money you're talking about."

He shook his head. "I set aside money for you, for your future wedding and a down payment for a house." When her jaw dropped, he winced. "I gather you didn't get it."

She shook her head. "No, I didn't get anything like that."

"What about student loans?"

"Well, I have them, and I'm paying them off," she replied. "Why?"

"Because there was money for your education as well." He turned and looked back up at the house. "Well, … shit's about to hit the fan. I'm afraid that the battle she's fighting is about to get a whole lot uglier."

"Whoa, whoa, whoa, hang on a minute." Risa raised her hands. "I really don't want to be a part of that."

"No, of course not," he replied, giving her a gentle smile. "You were always the best thing that came out of that relationship. I'm sorry I didn't get to spend more time with you."

"I wish that I had too," she said. "Just everything always seems so chaotic, you know, with relationships and all."

He nodded. "And it wasn't meant to be either," he noted gently, "and I can see how this has been a bit of a shock. Not to worry. I'll see what we can do about it."

"You don't need to do anything about it," Risa stated. "I never expected anything from anybody."

He chuckled. "And that's one of the reasons I'm more than happy to help out, but the money was given to Eleanor for you."

"Well, I certainly didn't see it," she declared, "and, if you want to check on my student loans, I'm sure there's a way for your lawyers to do that."

"You know there might be," Graham replied contemplatively, "and that was even something that Eleanor signed off on."

Risa winced. "I really don't want to get dragged into all that. It would just make everything else worse."

Graham gave her an awkward hug, then added, "If you ever want to do coffee or dinner or something, I would be more than happy to see you."

"I would love that," Risa shared. "Honestly, it's been such a tumultuous time that I haven't really had a chance to figure out what happened between you two."

"I think," he began, then hesitated and continued, "I suspect it's the same thing that's happened every time. Either she got bored or she just wanted more."

"Ah." Risa nodded. "I hate to say you're right, but you

probably are."

He chuckled. "I thought I understood who I was marrying, but I guess I didn't."

"I don't think anybody ever really understands my mother, including me," she shared, as she glanced back. "I just found out that somebody I cared about and encouraged to go into the military because it was something that he really needed to do for himself, called home several times to talk to me. She not only didn't pass on the messages, but I suspect she even went so far as to give him an earful. And she's never missed an opportunity to tell me what an awful loser he was and that I was better off to be rid of him. It's as if she was playing a game."

"I can see her doing just that," Graham muttered. "What did she say to him?"

"He's not letting on exactly all these years later. I thought that he didn't care, only to find out that he was steered off by her." She gave Graham a sad smile. "I just found out today that she had decided he wasn't good enough for me, and, because he didn't have money, he wasn't the person she wanted in my life. He's the only man I've ever loved too. I was devastated when I didn't hear from him."

"Oh no." Graham stared at Risa in horror. "That's not fair."

"No, it's not fair," she agreed. "I'm still feeling numb from the shock of it, though I guess I shouldn't be surprised, and it just makes me mad at myself."

"I am sorry to hear what she did. Remember though, your mother is damaged."

"I'm sure she is," Risa replied in fascination, as she stared at him, "and you appear to have come to terms with it."

"No, I really haven't," he noted, shaking his head. "I

have an awful lot of life still to come, but at one time I was prepared to do all kinds of things to make her life easier. Now I'm not interested."

Risa smiled and nodded. "No, of course not, and it's hard enough when you've been treated so badly. It's unforgiveable, really."

He handed her a business card and added, "You know where my office is. You've been there lots and are welcome anytime. Please don't be a stranger."

"Thank you," she said, with a wave and a smile.

As she got back into her car, her mother called her. Risa looked down at the number and shook her head, put her cell on Silent and drove away. The last thing she needed was to be interrogated by her mother over what her ex-husband had just told Risa.

Now she had to deal with the fact that Eleanor had taken money intended for Risa's own education and had squirreled it away for herself. When you talk about somebody having money issues, that's one thing, but when you talk about somebody having money issues and stealing from their own child, that was a whole different story.

Whatever was between Graham and Eleanor, they could sort it out on their own, and Risa wouldn't become a pawn, not after what her mother did to Cage.

CAGE MADE SEVERAL phone calls to set up the appointment to meet with Brian. Then Cage had to wait until after school was out. So, as he approached the foster home where Brian resided, Cage surveyed the neighborhood with a jaundiced eye. It was nice enough, but it felt almost too perfect. The house was too clean, with one of those spotless driveways, as if they cleaned, washed, and hosed it down daily, and in a way that was getting to him.

It wasn't fair, and it certainly was a quick judgment, but Cage couldn't stop from thinking this house was just an act, just a front, a façade. Maybe he was wrong, but there was no way to know that yet. As he walked up to the front door, he was greeted by a woman in full makeup and dressed to the nines. He introduced himself, but she remained silent. He hesitated, then asked, "I'm sorry. Are you on your way out?"

She frowned at him. "No. Is there a problem?"

He smiled and nodded, realizing he needed to get a grip on his attitude. "On no, thank you for seeing me."

She inclined her head gracefully and said, "I still don't quite understand what this is all about though."

He nodded, having told her in detail just a couple of hours ago. "Is Brian here?"

She hesitated and then replied, "Not yet, but he will be momentarily. My husband, Jameson, and I will sit in on the conversation." When Cage studied her steadily, she flushed. "I think it's only appropriate. We don't know who you are, and we don't know anything about what you're here for."

"As I mentioned in my earlier phone call, I'm here regarding his dog," he repeated carefully. "Surely that's not taboo."

"Well, of course it's not taboo," she huffed, staring at him intently, "but we don't want him upset."

"You mean, more upset than he already is?"

"Of course it's a terrible situation," she declared in exasperation.

"How long has he lived in your care?"

"It's been close to a month now," she replied.

"How is it working out?"

She stiffened and glared at him. "Are you from Child Services?"

"No, I'm not, but I will be headed there after this."

"Why?" she asked, frowning at him.

"Because it's part of my investigation, that's why." It was hard to keep the exasperation out of his tone. It was also hard to keep the judgment and the dislike out as well. He didn't know this person, and he really had no reason to dislike her, but just something about her mannerisms already had his teeth on edge.

She motioned to another room and said, "You can sit in the drawing room. I'll go make tea. Brian should be home anytime, and so will my husband," she added, with a stern look in his direction.

He nodded. "That's fine."

At that, she seemed to relax somewhat and headed into the other room.

Cage was pretty sure that, if he moved, even the slightest, she would have been there in a heartbeat. Again he felt this total sense of wrongness, of being in a very strange space that he didn't recognize as any home for a boy who lost his parents and his dog.

When a knock came on the door, it opened a few minutes later. Cage heard somebody talking in the other room. Brian was home. How many children moved so quietly and knocked when they got home? That thought alone unnerved him, and he frowned at that.

When the woman—her name was Dorothy—arrived a little bit later, she announced, "Brian is home now, but my husband is delayed." Cage nodded and waited. She hesitated, standing there, cracking her knuckles.

"I just want to talk to him about his dog," he repeated yet again. "You're more than welcome to sit in."

And, with a sense of relief on her face, she nodded. "I'll go get him."

When the boy rolled in a few minutes later, Cage noticed how comfortable he was in the wheelchair, and yet how tired he looked. "Hello, Brian," he greeted him, standing up and walking closer, holding out his hand. "I'm Cage." Brian shook his hand, staring up at him mutely. "Nice set of wheels," Cage added. The boy looked down at the wheelchair and shrugged, still stoic and silent. "My brother has a similar model, but he's got racing stripes down the sides."

The little boy's face lit up with some interest, but then it dove back down again fairly quickly. "Mrs. Mickey said you wanted to talk to me," he finally said, glancing over at her.

She nodded. "Yes, and, if you don't want to talk to him, that's fine too, and I'll ask him to leave."

Brian just shrugged.

It was almost as if everything was too much effort, or he just didn't care enough about anything, including being questioned. Cage's heart sank as he realized just how much the boy was struggling with his life right now. "I understand that you had a dog you cared about a lot."

His face beamed. "Scotty," he exclaimed. "I used to call him Scotty, after *Star Trek*," he muttered, and then his smile fell. He looked at Cage and asked, "Did you find him?"

"I haven't found him, but I am looking for him," he shared.

The little boy's eyes widened. "Are you? Because everybody I talked to told me that they hadn't seen him."

"I heard that too," Cage confirmed, "but he's a War Dog, which I'm sure you already know."

Brian nodded proudly. "My parents were really happy when we got him, and super happy we were such great buds." He beamed. "I really loved him." At that, his face twisted up with tears.

Dorothy barreled over quickly. "No baby tears. We don't cry in this house."

Brian took several shuddering sobs and looked down at the floor, as he worked to control himself. Finally he took a deep breath and looked back at Cage. "I would really appreciate it if you could let me know if he's okay," he stated formally.

Cage glanced back at Mrs. Mickey. "I don't know if you understand how close Brian and Scotty were."

"It doesn't matter," she stated. "It's a dog, and we don't have room here for a dog, not in this house."

Again the boy's face churned with emotion, and, for Cage, it was heartbreaking. "So that is your decision?" he asked, not expecting any answer. Cage looked to Brian. "You ever play any basketball?"

"Well, of course he hasn't," Dorothy interrupted, with a hard glare in his direction. "I mean, he's in a wheelchair obviously."

"I can see that, ma'am, but my brother is also in a wheelchair, and he plays a crazy game of basketball. He's played for some time and, in fact, is away at a basketball try-out camp right now."

Brian's face lit up. "Is it really possible to do that?" he asked, looking at his chair and then looking around.

"It absolutely is possible," Cage declared, "and, for somebody in a wheelchair, I'm sure there are all kinds of extra funding available to get you into something like that."

Immediately Dorothy glared at him. "That won't be

necessary. We will look after him just fine."

Cage turned to face her. "So, of course you're doing adaptive training for Brian, with extra physical work to keep his upper body in line with everything else he's going through? And you're making sure he's in sports that are particularly suited for a wheelchair, correct?" She stiffened and grimaced now. Undeterred, Cage added, "I'm just checking in to confirm he's getting *everything* that he needs."

She threw her hair back. "This is a trial period for all of us to see if it'll work out," she declared. "No one has made a decision on how that'll be, but you can bet that we do not have time or interest in having him go into sports only to be disappointed."

"Disappointed how?" Cage asked, staring at her.

"It's not as if he'll get very far, will he? He's handicapped," she stated with emphasis, "and adjustments must be made."

Cage stared at her for a long moment. "Brian certainly has challenges, but, given the right support, he can explore all kinds of opportunities and can find out more about what he is interested in pursuing. A smart, strong boy like Brian can excel in whatever he sets his mind to."

She glared at him. "I think it's time you left."

"Almost," he said casually. He looked back down at Brian. "Do you have any idea what happened to Scotty or when you last saw Scotty?"

He shrugged. "I was at home when they came to tell me about my parents," he began, his voice thickening. "I didn't even get a chance to pack my bags or anything. I was carted off without having any say in any of it," he murmured. "I kept calling for Scotty, but they kept saying that I couldn't take him where I was going and that he would be fine. They told me that somebody would look after him, but, every time I asked about him, nobody told me anything."

"And was it Child Services that took you away?"

Brian nodded. "They'd heard about the accident and came to pick me up," he replied, his bottom lip trembling.

"Where did you go from there?"

He shrugged. "To a place where other kids in wheelchairs were, but I didn't like it."

"Of course not," Dorothy stated. "It was an awful place. This is a much better home for him."

Brian looked as if he wanted to say something to that but clearly wasn't free to do so.

"Do you get to go out and to do all kinds of events here? Do you have friends to socialize with? Are you in a regular school?"

Brian nodded. "I'm in a regular school, and I have a school bus that takes me back and forth," he replied, red in his face. "But I do miss my friends, and I miss the people where I used to live. They all knew me, and it felt …" He hesitated, quickly glanced over at Dorothy. "Well, it felt like home."

"Of course it did, dear," Dorothy said. "That's what home is supposed to feel like."

Brian just nodded and didn't say anything more, but it's obvious that, for him, his world had changed in ways that he had no idea how to fix.

"I'm sorry," Cage told Brian. "That's a lot to deal with. Are you okay if I come back and talk to you again?"

His face lit up. "Yes, please, particularly if you can find out something about Scotty."

"That may take some time, but I needed to have some idea of where you last saw him. Then we could put some ideas together as to what happened to him. But I will definitely follow up and get answers one way or another."

At that, Brian's face fell. "Do you think he's dead?"

"No, I don't think he's dead at all," Cage declared, with a smile. "But that doesn't mean life is always sunshine and roses, or that we get the answers that we want," he added.

"No, we don't," Brian muttered. "I've already learned that. I wish more than anything that my parents could come home, but I guess that can't happen now."

"No, I'm sorry, Brian," Cage replied, "but that doesn't mean that life won't go on or that you can't carve yourself out a rewarding future still. I know it's hard to see that sometimes, particularly now," he explained gently, "but there are bigger and brighter days ahead for you."

The boy just nodded, but he didn't believe it, glancing back at the woman who was assigned to look after him.

Not everybody was prepared to deal with somebody in a wheelchair, and Cage hated to say it, but this woman acted as if this trial probably wouldn't end well.

Cage handed Brian a card and said, "Hang on to that, and, if you ever need me or need anything, you just give me a shout."

Brian looked over at Dorothy, who was staring at him, frowning.

"Obviously he won't need anything," she declared, "and you shouldn't be doing things like that with a child."

"If you say so," Cage quipped, putting a smile on his face. He stood up, smiled down at Brian, and knowing full well that life would send him more difficult events, Cage whispered, "Remember what I said." As he walked to the front door, he added, "I'll follow up on Scotty, honest. As soon as I find out something, I'll let you know."

Brian's face lit up again.

"It doesn't matter either way," Dorothy snapped. "He won't be allowed to have the dog, so it won't matter."

Cage stared directly at Dorothy. "I think everybody wants to know that their best friend when they were a child is now safe in some other place. It will probably help Brian adapt to being here a whole lot easier, if he knows that Scotty is safe."

Immediately Brian nodded. "I really want to know that Scotty's okay," he whispered.

Cage could hear the worry in his tone and the pain in his heart. He smiled at the boy, then nodded. "I'll let you know." And, with that, he let himself out. Without looking back, he headed to his vehicle. Only when he got into his vehicle and was out of sight did he realize how hard he was struggling to hold back the tears threatening to spill down his cheeks and the sobs choking his throat.

This wouldn't be easy. Brian was a fish out of water in that home, and that woman, for all her God-saving spirit and righteousness, simply was not a good fit for that boy. If they had no intention of showing Brian what a full life in a wheelchair could be like, he would stagnate and would never begin to access his full potential, not until he had a chance to leave that smothering atmosphere in that home.

Even then, a positive mind-set was so important when it came to adapting to and accepting his injury. Even though Cage didn't know what all Brian's disability required to give him a full life, Cage knew Brian needed someone who would help him far more than that Dorothy woman ever could.

Brian was in a wheelchair, and that wheelchair was an extension of himself. It was hard enough for the boy to have lived through everything he had endured so far, and, while he certainly wasn't alone in being dealt hardship after hardship, there also had to be good things in Brian's life, and it would be hard to find them in a house like that.

CHAPTER 5

R ISA WAITED NERVOUSLY for Cage to pick her up. He'd texted her earlier, looking for her address, and she'd spent the better part of the day fussing over what she would wear. She alternated between being furious at her mother and nervous about tonight. She had no reason to be nervous, yet it was a date—essentially a first date for two people who'd gotten sidetracked and had fallen out of touch for too many years, … all because of her mother. Thinking about the whole confrontation earlier made her angry all over again.

When the doorbell rang, she raced to the door, only nobody was there. Frowning, she stepped back into her apartment, wondering whether it had just been a mixed-up delivery or something else. She really didn't know. When it rang a second time, she took a little longer to answer, calling out, "Who is it?"

"It's me," Cage replied. When she opened the door and saw him, she smiled with relief. His eyebrows rose. "What happened?"

She shook her head, unsure of what to say. "I mean, it's nothing really."

"That's not an answer," Cage stated. "What happened?"

"Somebody rang the doorbell earlier, and, when I went to let you in, nobody was there."

"You didn't see anybody?" he repeated, as he stepped into the apartment, then stepped back out, looking down the hallway.

"I mean, an exit is right there, so it's possible I missed someone. I guess it could have just been me hearing things. We all get deliveries here pretty frequently, and mistakes are fairly common."

"Right," Cage muttered, as he glanced back out into the hallway, then looked back at her, smiled, and added, "It seems to have upset you. I'm sorry."

She winced. "It's just been that kind of a day."

He nodded. "Shall we go?"

"Absolutely," she murmured, as she followed him out to his vehicle, but she couldn't stop herself from glancing around.

"Are you expecting trouble?" He gently placed a hand on her lower back, easing her ahead of him ever-so-slightly.

"No, I'm not expecting trouble. It's just that … I had quite a row with my mother today, and, ever since, I feel the need to check behind me all the time." Then she added, "I also saw my latest stepfather for the first time in a very long while." She shook her head. "That was bizarre too."

"Bizarre how?" She told him about the money for college she'd never received, and the student loans she was still paying on to this day. He looked at her in shock. "She didn't give it to you?"

Risa shook her head. "No, and I haven't even braced her about that because I didn't know at the time. Apparently he also gave me money for my future wedding and a down payment on a house. It looks as if she apparently kept that too."

"Good God," he muttered.

"Hey, I'm impressed that you aren't already cussing her out."

"I think I'm still in shock," he muttered. "Just give me a minute."

She laughed. "I don't even know what to say. I have to admit it would have been really helpful to have had the school money, if only to cover my student loans. It's brutal out there in this world to try and get an education on your own, and I did get it, but not without incurring plenty of debt in the form of student loans. I'm working my way through them, but I certainly haven't paid them off yet."

"I don't think anybody would be surprised at that, not if they knew the situation," he murmured, "but if I didn't have a reason to hate her before …"

"You still don't," she said, then she hesitated. "She did admit she hadn't passed on the messages from you."

He nodded. "Well, that's what we figured already."

"I know, but it's just so upsetting to think she would deliberately do such a thing."

He glanced over at her. "You've always had such a nice view of her."

"No, I really haven't," she countered, raising her hands in protest. "I don't think I'm living in some Pollyanna world where I don't understand what she's done. I just hadn't realized the depth and breadth of her deception and animosity," she muttered. "I know money is her god and always has been, but I didn't think she would try to beat me out of something that many would consider her responsibility to provide for me to begin with."

"I'm sorry," Cage whispered. "Seems to be a bad deal all the way around."

"Agreed," she muttered. "On a happier note, it was nice

to talk to Graham, my stepfather. I really liked him. Hell, I liked most of her husbands,"

"How many were there?" Cage asked, looking at her curiously.

She frowned. "I think he was the sixth."

Cage shook his head. "Damn. And is she on the prowl for number seven?"

"I would imagine so, but apparently she's still tied up in some court cases—with Graham, at least—and those will likely get more complicated, now that he knows she kept money that wasn't hers."

"When it comes to marriage, a lot of times the money is not necessarily divided fairly, which leaves people trying to take the other to court."

"I don't know all the details, and I don't really want to. It's bad enough that I have to deal with her and all her nonsense involving me, but I really don't need to carry around the added burden of knowing all the other messed-up things she's done."

"Good," he said, as he opened the car door for her and let her slide in. Closing it behind her, he quickly went around and got in. "I thought maybe we would go for seafood."

She looked over at him and smiled. "I would absolutely love seafood."

"Good. It used to be one of your favorites."

"I haven't had very much of it," she said. "I've been focusing on paying my student loans, so I haven't been eating out much."

"And your beloved mother hasn't been helping."

"Nope, she's never been one to hand out money, even when I was young," Risa shared. "It was one of the things we fought about because she didn't understand why I went to college to begin with."

He looked at her, startled, taking his gaze briefly off the road, "Seriously?"

She nodded. "In her mind, I was supposed to just find a rich guy, get married, and settle down, right?"

"To me it sounds a little more like find a rich guy, milk him for all he has, and then settle down."

She winced. "That would be my mother's version, yes, but not mine."

He didn't say anything more, and she settled in quite happily for a pleasant drive to the restaurant.

"Are you okay?" he asked, when she snuggled down a little deeper into the seat.

"I'm doing fine. I just can't believe how much everything has shifted in these last few days." She looked over at him. "Were you able to connect with the little boy?"

"I did." He nodded and gave her a smile. "Brian is a sweet kid. He's quiet, obviously still dealing with the trauma, and sadly he's missing his dog pretty badly. He's not just missing the dog, he's worried about him too."

"Of course he is," she agreed. "That's got to be tough. How are the foster parents?"

He winced. "I'm not convinced that they're particularly well suited to fostering, especially not in Brian's case. He's capable of doing so much more than just sitting in a wheelchair, as Jason has proven so well, but not everybody believes it. I'm afraid if Brian doesn't get the kind of support that seeks opportunities, it will be harder on him to adjust."

"I'm surprised to hear that. If they're not the kind to take on the challenge, why would the family want to foster him? Most people would have to at least make some modifications to their house, maybe even get a different vehicle. Then you think about personal care and things like that, depending on his physical capabilities. It really does take a special person to do this and to do it well."

"I think so too," he agreed, "but they got him somehow. By the way, it's a perfect house, you know, one of those where you don't dare sit down for fear of messing something up."

"Oh, *ugh*." Risa shook her head. "That's not good for a child, especially one in a wheelchair."

"It's also a trial scenario, which Dorothy made very clear, in front of Brian no less, and I think that makes it even harder on him."

"Of course it does. Brian's got to be on his best behavior. Otherwise he'll get kicked out and moved on to who-knows-what," she exclaimed. "That sucks too. Hell, my mother used to pull that stunt on me all the time."

"What do you mean?" Cage asked, turning to her.

"She used to tell me that, if I didn't smarten up, she would make sure that her husband—and I don't remember which one it was at the time—would get rid of me because she didn't have the time or energy to deal with my tantrums." Risa shook her head at that. "Memories are so strange, and who knew that one was still rattling around in my head?" She laughed. "God, it all just seems like such a long time ago."

"And yet it probably wasn't," he noted. "I imagine that, in your mother's case, she would hold a grudge for a very long time."

"She holds more than just a grudge," Risa noted, with a smile. "I mean, this discussion today? … The gloves were off before I even got in the house, which is a story in itself. It's pretty depressing to even think that something like that is still happening in my world."

"Unfortunately it happens all the time," Cage said, with a sad smile.

"Sure, but you can't see that or don't realize it when you're all caught up in it yourself. I am obviously far better off without her in my life, but if my stepfather takes her to court over the student loans money and other money he set aside for me for a house, … my relationship with my mother will get even uglier."

"But that's not your fault," Cage declared. "If Graham handed over the money for you, and there's any documentation of it, and Eleanor used it on herself, the repercussions could be quite severe."

"In which case she really won't talk to me," Risa stated, looking over at him. "Graham did say something about a contract."

"Then your mother could be having a bigger headache than you ever thought," Cage said cheerfully.

He sounded so positively giddy about it that Risa stared at him and started to laugh. "You're totally okay if she gets into trouble over this, aren't you?"

"Oh, I so am," he confirmed, with a smile. "She's been a pretty shitty mother in so many ways, but to take money that was intended for your education and to help you buy a house, that's majorly shitty, even for her. And that is all on her, not you."

"And yet I'm sure she would say it was her money, rightly hers because she looked after me."

"Well, we'll see what the judge says about that," Cage noted, with a smile. "If it was me, I wouldn't be very happy if somebody was taking the money for her own use, especially if it was explicitly given for a particular reason."

Risa shook her head. "I told Graham that I didn't want to get involved and that I definitely didn't want to be part of their fight."

"What did he say to that?"

"He just smiled, patted my hand, and told me how he would love to take me out for dinner sometime or go for coffee."

"Good." Cage nodded. "Go, have fun with him, make some nice memories. It sounds like a relationship that probably would be good to have back in your life. I don't think Eleanor can control everything that goes on in your world, although she might give it a good try."

"Oh, she will give it a good try all right," Risa agreed, "but this time I'm pretty sure I have somehow managed to free myself from the worst of what she can do."

"I would hold on to that thought," Cage noted, with a grin, "because Eleanor? She's not somebody who will give up control easily."

"No, but she also can't have any control, if I don't give it back to her," Risa declared. "So here's to my freedom."

And, with that, she leaned over and kissed him gently on the cheek. "No matter what she did before, anything between me and you now? That's between us. She can go to hell."

CAGE WAS REALLY happy to hear Risa say these words and wondered just how strict she would be in the face of her mother's opposition. Eleanor had always been very abrasive, very formidable, and with a negative opinion on everything in life. If you didn't go along with her, you were either stupid or just too naïve to understand. It had been a very interesting experience meeting her for the first time, trying to decipher just who this character was and what her actual motivations were, because she had proven to be somebody you just couldn't take at face value.

It seemed as if she always had something on her back burner, some underhanded play going down that you would never be privy to.

One, because she wouldn't ever let you into her inner circle; and, two, because you were just not good enough. He never figured her out, so maybe it was just because he was male. He didn't know what her deal was, but, considering how she treated her own daughter, that was probably only part of it. Definitely a power play, from somebody who liked to be in control. Definitely some narcissistic tendencies were there, but, as long as Risa was doing well and staying free and clear of Eleanor's grasp, that alone would change Risa's life quite a bit. He could hope for the best.

As he pulled into the restaurant parking lot, she cried out in joy. He looked over and smiled. "It's almost as if you haven't been here before."

"I haven't been here in …" She stopped and frowned. "Well, not since you left. And never in this location."

His eyebrows shot up. "Seriously?"

She nodded. "After you left, I just focused on school, and life became one endless round of exams and assignments and then just work itself," she explained, with a shrug. "It wasn't an easy time for me either."

"I'm sorry to hear that," he replied, frowning.

She shook her head. "We're here now, together. So we'll start afresh and figure out just where we're at," she stated in a noncommittal tone. "I've changed. You've changed, but …" She studied the restaurant in front of them and beamed. "Apparently this place hasn't changed."

"Do you still like clam chowder?" he asked with a smile, as he unlocked the car doors and got out.

She hopped out on her own and walked up several steps, where she stopped, faced him, and grinned. "Absolutely, and lobster rolls," she added. "Although I don't think this place has them." She looked up at the rather daunting front entranceway that showed a lot of class and had a regal look to it. "I feel as if this place has been around forever, and maybe that I am underdressed."

"I remember it way back when," he replied, "so that's a good thing. That means they're also used to all kinds of people, so don't you even begin to feel as if you're not dressed properly. You look beautiful."

She glanced down at her clenched hands and sighed. "I haven't really done a whole lot of dating or even going out to meals with girlfriends," she explained. "My workload has been pretty intense."

"I imagine it was, but you got yourself a good education and in a field that is wide open and always in need," he noted. "You should be proud of yourself."

She smiled. "I am. I absolutely am, and it also gave me the freedom to move out, so … I'm still dealing with a lot of student loans."

"Right"—he gave her an eye roll—"and we know why."

She winced but gave him a half laugh. "We'll ignore that topic for the moment. Obviously some things would have made my life easier, but I got through it on my own, and I'm not sad about that."

"Good."

As they walked in, they were greeted by a hostess. When Risa realized he'd made a reservation, she looked over at him, with one eyebrow raised.

"I wasn't sure how busy it would be," he said, by way of explanation. "So it just seemed to be the easiest answer."

It absolutely was the easiest answer, but it also meant that he had taken it upon himself to make reservations in the hope that she would agree to come with him. He didn't want to admit that, but, from the expression on her face, surely he knew that she'd already put two and two together. "I always heard how it's fairly tough to get into here," she whispered, as they were led to a table.

"Exactly," he agreed. "Hence, the reservation."

She smiled as they were seated at a lovely table with a view. She gave a happy sigh, as she stared out at the city around them. "It really does feel as if something has suddenly changed in my world," she murmured.

"It has," he confirmed, looking over at her, a big smile on his face. "Think about it. You stood up to your mother, and you've potentially reconnected with your stepfather, with whom you were close for quite a few years. And, even though you found out some terrible things about your mother that are hurtful and disappointing, you also braced her about it. Thus, you are no longer the victim in the face of her betrayals."

Risa nodded. "That's a good way to put it."

They enjoyed a wonderful seafood dinner, getting to know each other again. When the time came to order dessert, Risa shook her head and patted her tummy. "I have absolutely no more room."

"How about an after-dinner drink?" the waitress suggested.

Risa shook her head. "Not me. I'm sorry. I'm full." She looked over at Cage. "What about you? Do you still have that sweet tooth?"

"I do, he admitted, with a smile, "but I think I'm good. We'll just take the check, please." The waitress disappeared, just as his phone rang. He looked down at it and frowned, not recognizing the number.

"Go ahead," Risa encouraged him. "I know that you're here for a specific reason, and there's no reason to miss an important call just because we're out together."

He looked at her and smiled. "A lot of women wouldn't be quite so generous."

She shrugged. "Ah, but remember, I'm not *a lot of women*."

He chuckled, as he answered the phone, "Hello?" He heard a sob on the other end. "Hello? Who is this?"

A faint whisper said, "It's me, but if you tell them, … I'm in trouble."

Cage knew who it was. "Brian, is that you?"

"Yes," he whispered. "Did you find out anything about Scotty?"

"Not yet, buddy. I'm working on it though."

Choking back a sob, Brian added, "It hurts. … It hurts so bad."

"I'm so sorry," Cage replied. "You've had a hell of a shift in your life, and I'm sure it's been pretty tough on you."

"They don't like me," he muttered.

Cage stared at the phone for a moment and asked, "Why would you say that?"

"It's true."

"And yet they don't need to take you into their home," Cage noted. "To be a foster parent is a choice, and they made that choice."

"I don't think so," Brian argued. "I don't know how it works, but I don't think … It doesn't seem as if they *have* a choice."

Cage frowned at that and asked, "Aren't you happy there?"

After a silent moment, Brian said, "They don't hurt me."

Cage saw that as an opening line that begged so many more questions. At the same time, it hurt his heart to even think of anybody hurting someone who was already so vulnerable. "Have other people hurt you?" Cage asked, his voice a little sharper.

More silence came on the other end for a moment and another sob. Then Brian answered, "Not so much hurt, but …"

"Right," Cage acknowledged. "There are a lot of ways that people can be hurt." The little boy, with his quiet sobs, was enough to break Cage's heart. "Was there any other foster family you could go to?"

"Maybe, but, even if there was, it doesn't mean it would be any better."

"That's true. What about going back to the center where you were before?"

"I don't know," he muttered. "At least other people like me were there."

"It's important to have people like you around, isn't it?"

"It makes it easier," he whispered. "They understand. Sometimes I …" He hesitated, then continued, his words coming out in a rush. "Sometimes I have accidents."

"Of course you do," Cage replied. "That's just part of adjusting."

"They don't like it."

"Well, it doesn't matter whether they like it or not. It's a fact of life," Cage told the little boy. "Remember how I told you that my brother was in a wheelchair? It took quite a while for him to get control enough to not have accidents sometimes."

"Did he get there?" Brian asked, with such hope in his tone that it made Cage cringe all over again.

"Yes, he sure did, and he plays basketball now, and he does really well."

"Wow. I tried to look up that stuff on the internet, but I guess I'm not allowed. They don't like it because it gives me bad ideas."

"I'm sorry they feel that way, but I don't think they are bad ideas. I would hope it gives you a variety of ideas and the confidence to try new things and to stretch a little bit," Cage shared. "It's not easy when you're first in a wheelchair. It's not always easy when you've been in a wheelchair for a while, but your circumstances have changed drastically, and I don't know that a lot of people understand that."

"They don't. Not at all. It would help a lot if they would."

"Understood," Cage replied. "Did you need me for something specific," he asked hesitantly, "or did you just need to talk?"

Brian sobbed slightly. "I need Scotty."

"Of course you do," Cage agreed. "But you do understand that, even if I find Scotty, it'll be a challenge to see him if you are living where you're at, right?

"I know," he said, "but I need to know he's okay. He was a good dog, and he really looked after me." His crying was audible again. "It would help to know he's still out there somewhere."

Cage glanced over at Risa, tears in her own eyes. He grabbed her hand. "There will be better days, Brian," he murmured. "Sometimes we just have to reach a little deeper to find it."

"I don't think any good days remain in this world anymore," Brian mumbled. "I just want Scotty, and I want my family back."

"I can't do anything about your family," Cage stated, "but I'll do everything I can to try and find Scotty."

"Promise? And you won't give up?"

"I promise, Brian. I won't give up." Now Cage was desperately trying to keep his voice from cracking.

Brian ended the call on that note, and hopefully now could get some sleep. Cage looked to Risa, biting her bottom lip to keep from crying.

"Dear God," she whispered, staring at Cage, "that just tears me apart."

"It tears me apart too," Cage admitted. "Nobody ever thinks about the pets when it comes to these situations. They're secondary problems. I can't really blame the first responders. When something deadly happens, their major focus is all about treating the people. The trouble is, in many cases, treating the people also means treating the animals they were close to. In Brian's case, he's obviously suffering terribly."

Risa asked, "You can find the dog, right?"

He looked over at her and nodded. "I'm doing what I can in terms of locating Scotty. I'm waiting for some phone calls to be returned. Also remember that I just met this little boy today."

"And I've been dragging you away from it all," she moaned. "Let's go. Come on. We can leave now, and maybe you can make some more phone calls or do whatever you need to do."

He gave a bark of laughter, as the waitress returned just then with their bill. He quickly paid it and then escorted Risa outside. "Tomorrow I'm meeting with Child Services and the police. I was supposed to meet today but ran out of time so had to reschedule."

"Why the police?" Risa asked.

"Because they should have opened a file on the little boy, and it should have something in it as to what happened to the dog. If Scotty was taken to a shelter, hopefully we can find out which one, and they should know what happened to him."

"Right." Risa frowned. "I didn't even consider what happens to these poor animals when someone's life goes to hell like this."

"And that's a problem," Cage noted. "Nobody really does, and it's hard for these kids. It's so hard, and we have to find a way forward regardless."

"Jesus," Risa muttered, just listening to him.

"I know," Cage replied. "Brian's quite a kid, but he's very quiet, which is worrisome. I think in many ways he feels torn apart."

"Well, he has been torn apart," she agreed, looking back at Cage. "You remember how you felt when your brother ended up in the wheelchair. Imagine if he hadn't had someone like you and your mom."

"My mom?" he repeated, with an eye roll.

"For a while there she was decent," Risa reminded him.

"Yes," he conceded, "she was, and that made a big difference to Jason. So you're right."

"This little guy's got nobody."

"I know," Cage muttered, "but the thing is, he's not alone. A lot of wheelchair-bound kids are out there."

She shook her head at that. "You think that you should do something about that too?"

"Well, it's certainly something I'll consider now, but I just don't know quite what one is supposed to do about it." He looked over at her and asked, "What about you?"

"That's nothing I had ever considered, but, like you, I question how people just let this go by without looking at what the options are," she replied.

"Oh, I get it, but there aren't any good options, not in Brian's case, not with his current foster parents. Somebody else has to take on the responsibility of raising him and helping him adjust."

She looked over at him. "That would be a good job for you."

"*Right*." Cage gave her an eye roll. "A good job for a single guy, dealing with my own disabilities. I don't think anybody would let me have him."

"You don't know that," she argued, "and then there's Jason. I'm sure he would be all over it."

Cage laughed. "Honestly, Jason would probably be Brian's biggest supporter. Hell, he would be the best person I could possibly have to stand up for me too, ... but that doesn't mean it's the best answer for Brian, not in the eyes of Child Services."

"No, it might not be, but, every time I think about what that little boy is going through"—she shuddered—"I find it traumatizing. So I can't imagine how anybody else doesn't feel the same. What do you think he meant when he told you that his foster parents may not have had a choice?"

"I'm not sure." Cage thought back to the fancy furniture

and the stately property. "It could be about the money. If they're living above their means, maybe this is how they are trying to maintain their lifestyle and their status quo."

"Yeah, but they won't get a whole lot of money for looking after him, would they?"

"Oh, I'm sure they get more looking after a disabled child," he pointed out.

She winced. "That is a terrible reason to foster a child."

"Maybe so, but then again, is Brian better off there, or is he better off in some home?"

"Like a group home or an institution?" Risa shuddered. "Things like this remind you just how lucky you are to be who you are and to have what you have," she shared. "This is a good day for me to get that reminder."

"You've done well today, considering," Cage said, as they got into the vehicle, and he drove her home. "Just remember that I'm doing what I can to help him right now. Even as I drop you off, I'll go past Brian's former home again because I'm not sure what's going on there—particularly after something I saw today."

"What did you see?"

"Nothing concrete," he replied, "just something that's off."

"Well, a lot of things are off in this world, but, if you want to know anything about the neighborhood, apparently Celine's newest boyfriend might have answers."

"Or he is the cause," he pointed out, as he turned into Risa's apartment complex.

She winced at that. "That wouldn't be very nice."

"No, maybe not, but I'll do some research and then walk the area. So, I'm heading back to get a few hours in tonight. It feels as if I'm getting nowhere quickly." He parked near her main entrance.

"If there's anything I can do to help, you let me know," Risa stated, as she got out.

He stepped out to give her a hug. "I will, but I obviously won't let this go anytime soon."

"Good, and I mean it. If there's anything I can do, you let me know. That little boy needs to have a better answer than what he's been given so far. That poor dog too," she added. "Why does nobody ever care about the animals?"

"I don't know that they *don't* care about animals as much as they don't really understand just how traumatizing it is for the animals as well as the humans. It's not in everybody's thought process, so the animals tend to get forgotten. They go to a shelter, and, if they're lucky, they get adopted again. The animals are expected to forget their families because nobody ever thinks about the bond that they have with the kids either."

"It's awful," she declared. "You go do what you gotta do."

He smiled and gave her a gentle kiss. "I'll call you in the morning."

She stared up at him and nodded. It looked as if she wanted to say something and then shrugged. "Call me," she murmured.

And, with that, he walked her up to her front door and made sure she got inside. Once she had the door locked, he turned and headed back to his vehicle.

He absolutely wouldn't let that little boy down, even if that meant Cage needed to find out a whole lot more about what had happened to Brian's family, and, more important, what had happened to Scotty.

He drove back to a rental house in the same neighborhood as Brian used to live in, where Cage brought out his laptop and started searching. Badger had also emailed another folder to Cage. He went through what appeared to be the police file, or at least a good portion of the police file, researching the details on what had happened to Brian's family. It had been a hit-and-run accident, but it also seemed that they had been targeted, as a vehicle had been seen following behind them for a while.

Apparently Brian's mother, Fiona, had been on the phone with her sister, Portia, who commented to the police that her sister mentioned that somebody was following them and that they couldn't seem to shake the tail. Fiona had tried to make it seem to be a joke, but she could tell that her sister was worried.

Cage had to wonder why the sister hadn't taken in her nephew, a question that he would have no problem asking. He called and made an appointment to see Portia the next day. She'd been quite surprised to hear from him, but that's okay. Cage needed to get to the bottom of all this and the sooner, the better.

After he had gone through the police file and had a better understanding of what had gone on with that murder investigation, he reached out to the cop, a Detective Hendricks, who had provided the information to Badger. When Cage got a return phone call about forty minutes later, Hendricks was surely pissed.

"I don't want any of your team involved in this."

"I understand that," Cage replied in a mild tone, "but I also just visited Brian, who is really upset and rather desperate to know that his dog is safe."

Hendricks paused and asked, "That's really all you're here for?"

"Yes, I'm here because of the War Dog."

"God," Hendricks mumbled, "to think the government has money for this shit."

"You don't like dogs?" Cage asked, trying for a neutral tone of voice.

"Of course I like dogs, and, when these things happen, it's a bad deal for everybody. And, if there isn't family to take the dog, it can be even harder on the family. I'm just referring to the budget and all that."

"Good to know. So, in this case, what happened to Scotty, the War Dog?"

"I don't know," he admitted. "My understanding is they would pick him up, but we haven't got any confirmation that they did."

"Who would that be?"

Hendricks stated, "Animal Control. If they picked him up, they would have taken him to a shelter. However, if he wasn't adoptable, … they would have put him down."

"Christ," Cage swore. "To think of all the government money and training that went in these animals, not to mention the fact that they've served our country and have saved countless lives, how can they then get caught up in this? Does nobody even check? Do they just get put down without a care?" Cage asked in shock.

"I can't know for sure, as they didn't find him initially. I'm just telling you that it's quite possible."

"Well, it sure as hell better not have happened," he snapped. "A little boy in a wheelchair, who's already been through hell after losing his parents and getting some cold foster parents, is pretty desperate to know that his best friend in the whole wide world is doing okay."

"How is the boy doing?"

"Not great, which is to be expected to a degree, and adjustments have to be made, which I understand," Cage acknowledged, "but I don't think his current placement is a good fit, though I'm not sure there are too many options for him."

"Exactly. I know the Child Services folks weren't impressed at the time because they figured he had family, and it would be okay. However, if no family members are stepping up, it's a whole different ball game."

"Then what?" Cage asked. "Then it's foster care?"

"Or an institution. If nobody will take him into general care, then what are they supposed to do?" Hendricks blasted. "We don't have anything in place for kids like him. It's bad enough when we have as many foster kids as we do, but, when you get somebody with special needs, it's even harder."

"Yet he's just in a wheelchair. He doesn't have any mental deficiencies, personality disabilities, or anything," Cage noted. "You would think there would be something for Brian."

"Yeah, you would think so," the detective agreed, "but I've been in this business a long time, and I can tell you there isn't a whole lot of good news when it comes to these cases. I've seen too many in my lifetime to hold out hope anymore."

"So, you can't tell me anything more about the dog or where it would have gone?"

"No, all I can tell you is that we called Animal Control, which is standard protocol for us. You would have to contact them."

"I will. That'll be my first call in the morning."

"I'm surprised, being such an animal lover, that you didn't call them right away."

"I did, and I left a message, but I got no answer," he explained, frowning into the phone.

"Yeah, unfortunately that's a problem we're always up against too," the detective noted. "With so little manpower and so little budget, everybody is strapped. Remember that whenever you talk to someone," he added. "We're all doing the best we can with limited resources." And, with that, he disconnected.

Just as Cage was getting ready for bed, his phone rang again. He answered it, recognizing Risa's number. "What's the matter?" he asked.

A hoarse whisper came on the other end. "I think somebody is outside my place."

He frowned. "As in?"

"As in peeping in my windows. Can you come?"

"I'm on my way," he said, all thoughts of sleep gone from his mind.

CHAPTER 6

RISA STAYED HIDDEN behind the curtain for the next twenty minutes, hoping against hope that Cage would get here sooner than later. She didn't know what the hell this guy wanted, who he even was, or why he decided on her place as some place to sit and to pry into, but it was unnerving to say the least. When she'd seen the face in her window, she'd screamed out loud, and he had disappeared. She thought maybe he was gone for good, but, as she peered out the windows, she'd seen someone sneaking around the back.

She was on the second floor and that alone should have been enough of a deterrent, which is why she'd chosen a second-floor unit in the first place. But she also knew that plenty of guys could get in and out of apartment buildings without any trouble. Considering that she'd already had somebody knocking on her door earlier, only to find nobody there when she'd opened the door, was enough to unnerve her all over again.

When her phone buzzed with a text, she recognized it as Cage, reporting that he was outside and heading up. Clearly he was trying to prevent her from freaking out when he knocked on the door. She let out her pent-up breath slowly as she waited nervously for him to come. She felt such a sense of relief that he was here, but he wasn't here, not yet, and that was the part that would drive her nuts until he arrived.

As soon as the doorbell rang, she headed over and called out, "Who is it?"

"It's Cage," he replied loudly. She quickly opened up her door and threw herself into his arms. He held her close, nudging her inside, so he could close her door again. "Hey," he whispered. "It's okay. Just hold tight."

He got the door locked again and then pulled her to the couch, sat down, and just held her. She wasn't crying, but apparently she was mumbling something, generally sounding like an idiot. Embarrassed and yet too relieved to care, she pulled back, looked up at him, and whispered, "Oh God, I am so relieved you are here."

"Did you recognize him?"

She shook her head. "No, I didn't, and he didn't have a mask on, but he was looking directly in my windows."

Cage frowned at that, looking over at the windows. "Are you okay if I go out and take a look?" She clutched him tighter, and he frowned. "I do need to check, to confirm somebody isn't out there."

"But what if he is out there?" she asked. "What if he goes after you?"

He smiled. "That would be okay by me. I haven't had a workout since I left home."

She stared at him and shook her head. "No, no, no, you can't go out there and fight him."

"Yeah, I wasn't planning on fighting him," Cage clarified, "but bringing him in and calling the cops while I hold him in place? That's a different story."

"Call them about what? You know how weak the laws are these days. A Peeping Tom basically gets a slap on the wrist for a first-time offense, if they even bother with that.

Then they just leave him to continue on and to terrorize us some more."

"Which is why they do it," Cage agreed with a nod, "but that doesn't mean they get to continue. We also have to figure out whether this is deliberate or random."

"God, I don't even want to think about it being deliberate."

"Well, I don't think it's any nicer to think it's random either," he noted. "We just need to know who it is and put a stop to it. So, I want you to sit here quietly, and I promise I'll be back in a few minutes." With that, he got up and headed to the front door and whispered to her, right behind him, "Lock it behind me."

She nodded and slammed it shut. She hated to even send him out there, but he was also adamant that he would go, so what else was she supposed to do?

She groaned as she walked over to the window and kept an eye on what was going on outside, but she still remained hidden. That was about the only way she would keep an eye on anything out there. It was so damn scary.

On the other hand, not being able to see anything also was unnerving, so she kept looking and pulling back, then looking again and feeling like a fool. When Cage texted to say he was coming back in, she raced to the door, then waited and let him in. "Did you see anything?" she asked.

"No, nothing obvious, and nobody is out there now," he replied. "That doesn't mean they weren't there before or that they won't come back," he stated calmly. She gasped at that. He looked at her, then shrugged. "It all depends on what he's after," he pointed out, "and what he found. It makes a difference as to whether he'll also be here because it's a targeted attempt to find out who's living here or if somebody already knows that it's you."

Risa shook her head in panic. "God, that's very unnerving."

"Did you see a face?"

She nodded. "Why?"

"Well, because you're on the second floor," he pointed out gently.

"I know. I understand that, and I know it sounds foolish, but, yes, it was a face in my window," she declared. "And my balcony is right next to the one beside me."

He headed to the balcony and turned on the light, then stepped outside and nodded. "A fire escape is right along the corner too, so it wouldn't take too much to come up here. Interesting design."

"Yeah, not such a great design as far as I'm concerned," she muttered. "I mean, if they can come right up here, what's the point of being on the second floor?"

He nodded slowly, as he studied the area. "And it would appear that he could because I don't see any great hindrance to anybody who'll persevere and who is reasonably fit," he added, as he stared at the configuration of balconies. "It wouldn't take all that much to climb up."

"*Great*," she muttered, "that's not helpful."

"Maybe not, but it is definitely something we can't discount," he noted, turning to her.

"Where are you staying anyway?"

"A block away from the house where Brian's family used to live," he shared, looking over at her. "That was deliberate on my part."

"I didn't realize you were there, so close by."

"I wanted to keep an eye on it, just to see what was going on in the area, if anything is," he noted. "The fact that somebody says Brian's parents were murdered and that the police are keeping an eye on the house too, it just seemed like I should be closer."

"Right." She gave a headshake. "Somehow it never occurred to me that you would want to be closer."

He smiled. "It's not so much wanting to be closer, but wanting to get to the bottom of this."

"You don't think the dog is still running around free, do you?"

"I don't know," he admitted. "Yet it's possible. They certainly come back to what they know, and, if Scotty was in a place where he was happy or where he was desperate to come back and find Brian, Scotty could easily be returning to Brian's former home."

"It's been months though, hasn't it?" she pointed out.

He gave her a ghost of a smile. "Well, a month at best," he replied. "Yet, just like many animals, they can be very persistent in trying to sort out where their family has gone. So, I won't give up on the dog yet. If he's in a good home, and he's happy, and he has somehow found some peace with the fact that the little boy may be gone, or at least gone from his control, that's a whole different story."

She nodded. "The dog could be in another home and quite happy."

"I've made several phone calls to the shelter that supposedly was called to take him, but nobody's answered yet."

"And don't tell me that you go out wandering at nighttime, looking for him."

"Yes," he noted, with a smile, "I did go out looking."

Frowning, she stared at him. "You know it's dangerous."

He burst out laughing. "The thing is, it's dangerous no matter where you go. I'm not exactly a choir boy, and I have quite a bit of military training," he reminded her, shaking his head. "So, yes, in a way, it's dangerous, but it's not necessarily any more dangerous than anything else I do."

She shook her head. "Men are just very different creatures."

He chuckled. "That we are. Now, why don't you go back to bed, and I'll stay on the couch and confirm you're safe for the night."

She stared up at him. "The trouble is, … the night doesn't make me feel any better."

"Then maybe we need to look at moving you to a safer place," he suggested. "You have the right to feel safe in your own home."

She glanced at the window and shuddered.

He added, "Go on. It's fine. Get some sleep, and we'll talk tomorrow morning."

She nodded and slowly made her way back to her bedroom. It was terrible to feel so grateful that he was here. However, she had been unhappy and so seriously worried that it was hard to even imagine that she would drop off to sleep again. But it seemed as if she had absolutely no problem, once she realized that he intended to stay and fell into a deep, sound sleep.

When she woke up early the next morning, she instantly remembered and bolted from her bed, racing into the living room. There she found Cage up and about, already talking on the phone, fully dressed and sipping coffee. It took her a moment to reassess just where she was at and then grabbed herself a cup of coffee from the pot, as she sat down on the couch and waited for him to get off the phone.

She wasn't sure whether it was his boss or somebody else Cage was talking to, but the discussion was a serious conversation. When he finished the call, she looked over at him. "Problems?"

"Not necessarily but nobody seems to know where Scotty is. The shelter admits that they brought him in, but he disappeared almost immediately. They tried to hide it, unsure if it would be a problem or not. Seems it's a small shelter and not very sophisticated, not very well equipped or very well staffed. They had been told it was a War Dog because Brian told anyone who would listen, but they hadn't really believed him. The chip, however, confirmed it."

"So how did they lose him?"

"They apparently had the dog out for some exercise, just a walk around the block, and he got away from them and took off. They haven't seen or heard anything of him since."

"Any chance he's still hanging around?"

"I wouldn't be at all surprised," Cage replied, staring off in the distance.

She watched him, realizing the wheels were turning in his head. However, he just wasn't quite ready to tell her. "I can see that something's going on in your brain."

He smiled at her. "It's not so much that something's going on. It's just that Scotty has limited options."

"I know, and that worries me."

"Worries for his sake, or worries for Brian's sake?"

"Both. I love animals. You know that."

He nodded. "Jason called too, and I gave him an update on what I was doing. He was pretty outraged at the little boy's plight."

"Of course he would be," Risa replied gently "If anybody could understand where Brian was at, it would be Jason."

"I can imagine it myself to some degree, and I don't have the same physical limitations that he has. And frankly Jason doesn't have very many," he stated, looking at her. "Obviously there are some, but he has done phenomenally well."

"I'm really glad," she said. "Every time I see him, he blows me away—if for no other reason than he's just so positive and happy."

"He also has a girlfriend. Did I tell you that?"

She smiled at him and then shook her head. "You didn't tell me that, but good for him and good for her. Not necessarily an easy role, but not a hard one either, once you're all in."

"I think that's the trick, the all-in part," Cage declared, with a smile. "Of course you'll be happy to hear that Jason also adamantly demanded that I bring Brian home."

"What do you mean by home?"

"Really, you have no idea?" he asked, with a laugh. "My brother thinks we would make great foster parents."

"Will they let you?"

"I have no idea." Cage had to chuckle at the thought. "I can't see that it's even something we could contemplate, just because of our lifestyles. And surely Social Services would want somebody employed full-time. They certainly wouldn't consider a sixteen-year-old as an adult for purposes of adopting or fostering. So it would have to be me." He rolled his eyes. "That's a whole different commitment too."

"Of course it is," she agreed, staring at him, "but it does say an awful lot about Jason."

"What it says is that he feels as if Brian would have a much better life if he were around Jason, so Brian could get support and could see the possibilities."

"I won't argue that, but I think it would be the same for anybody with the same experiences as Jason."

"Exactly, and so, in his mind, it's *why not him*. I also told him that I ran into you."

"What did he say to that?" she asked hesitantly.

"I think he was happy. He basically told me, *It's about time.*"

She winced. "Yeah, and who knew? I just carried on with my world after the initial hurt had died down. I didn't really let myself think about it. I just went and got an education."

"I'm glad to hear that," Cage said, "because that is the best answer. When you don't know what's going on, and you don't have anything else for answers, you should just pick up and carry on," he shared. "So that was the right thing to do."

"I should have tried to reach you," she replied, "but I didn't. I didn't trust you enough, and I should have."

"No need to rehash any of that," Cage noted, with a smile. "We're already past that."

"Maybe, but I do have to examine who and what I was and why that was an okay thing to do. I had no reason *not* to contact you, except that you didn't contact me," she shared, with a shrug, "and that feels very selfish."

"Or very immature or very insecure. Pick a word, but really, does it matter?"

She frowned. "It should matter."

"No, it shouldn't," he countered. "Just because we all have traumas in our past doesn't mean we need to relive them in order to let them go. … Just decide to let them go. We don't have to go through that pain twice. Nobody says that we have to torture ourselves to redeem ourselves. We just move on knowing that, next time, we'll do the best we can to not end up in the same situation." She stared at him, her mouth hanging open. He laughed. "Yes, I've gone through therapy, lots of it." He rolled his eyes. "In case you couldn't tell."

"Yes, I can tell, … and it looks pretty good on you."

He smiled at that. "Good."

"So now what? You can't go to the shelter because they don't have the dog, and they have no records of the dog?"

"They have records of it, but they don't have any follow-up as to what happened to it. The guy I spoke to was gonna send me a copy of what he had in an email, but I haven't got that yet."

"Do you trust him?"

"No, trust is a tough one for something like this, but do I believe him. I would like to think that somebody there would tell us the truth, but, if somebody did something that hurt Scotty or if the way they lost him was grossly negligent or if in any way they feel as if they'll get charged or in trouble over it, I expect they will all lie," he admitted, with a smile in her direction. "It's human nature to protect ourselves."

"Well, it sucks," she declared, "because people need answers, particularly one little boy."

CAGE GLANCED OVER at Risa. "I'll need to leave." And he walked over, pulled her into his arms, and gave her a big hug. With a gentle kiss, he asked, "Will you be okay?"

"I want to come with you," she said, and he stopped and frowned. She shook her head, then gave him a small smile. "I've got the day off, … several days off, and I would like to come."

"It could be bad."

"I know it could be bad," she replied, "but, if you're looking for a dog and if we're trying to help a little boy, I want to help. Besides, I want to take you out for breakfast."

He rolled his eyes at that. "I want to do a walk around the property first."

"Good enough. We might even see Celine."

"Maybe," he said reluctantly.

"It's a good idea, and you should be happy."

He gave a bark of laughter. "I'm always happy to spend time with you," he muttered. "It wasn't why I came to town, but …"

"I know it wasn't," she noted. "I still think it's a good idea though. Besides, we only have a few days. You're here for however long and then you're gone."

He nodded, and that didn't make her feel any better.

Risa and Cage stopped off at one of the little breakfast places and had a quick meal. "You weren't very hungry?" she asked him, as they got back outside.

"No, I'm still pretty full from last night."

She nodded. "You're also walking with a bit of a limp this morning."

He glanced at her and shrugged. "I didn't take off my prosthetic last night, so it's a little sore."

She stopped and stared at him. "I'm so sorry. I didn't even think of that."

"Not yours to think about," he muttered. "That's on me."

Risa shook her head. "You were a guest at my house, and you came over to help me. Plus, I am a physical therapist. The least I could have done was offered you a little more care than that."

He shrugged. "I don't need more care."

There was the slightest bite to his tone, yet she understood it. Nobody really wanted to have their disability discussed like this. She frowned at him.

He raised his hand. "I'm fine. I just need to take it off tonight and spend some time without it to give my leg a bit of a break."

"Fine," she muttered, "be stubborn."

He laughed. "I will be just as stubborn as I've always been."

"*Great.* I'd forgotten that side of you."

"I'm sure you'll remember it soon enough," he quipped. They walked up the sidewalk, and he stopped, turned, and looked around several times.

"What is it you're looking for?" she asked curiously.

He frowned, then shrugged. "I don't know exactly. I'm just looking." As they got closer to the front door of Brian's former home, Cage thought he heard a dog in the distance. He stopped again, his ears keenly listening.

She asked, "That was a dog, wasn't it?"

"Yes, but that doesn't mean it was Scotty."

"No, of course not. I'm sure lots of people have dogs around here."

He nodded. "No doubt. Lots of people enjoy having a family dog."

"Of course nobody ever makes arrangements for who should get the dog if something happens to them, do they?"

"I don't think it's generally something that most people think of," Cage noted, "but that's hardly my issue today." As they walked up to the front door, he felt an eeriness to the place. Maybe because it was empty, or maybe because he knew that the family had died and their little boy desperately wanted to be back here with them.

"It feels sad, doesn't it?" she asked. "Everything seems overgrown, deserted. I suppose everything is still caught up in probate and all." She stopped and looked at him. "But everything should be Brian's, shouldn't it?"

He shrugged. "In theory, but I don't know what the parents' will says, and I don't know who the trustee is, since the boy is a minor."

"Somebody should be looking after him."

"Maybe, but *looking after him* sometimes means *losing an inheritance*," he pointed out.

Risa asked, "Nobody would have killed the family to get the house, would they?" He stopped, then looked at her, and she winced. "Right, stupid question."

"People do all kinds of shit and regularly kill for a lot less than a house," he shared. "So that's something we can never really let go of."

"It really sucks though," she muttered. "Brian's such a great kid, and anyone should be happy to have him as part of their family."

"They would if they were prepared to take on his disabilities," Cage added, "but not everybody is, though it's mostly out of ignorance. Ignorance and fear."

She just shook her head at that, and he smiled and kept on walking. As they got up to the front door, she muttered, "Too bad we can't go in."

With that, he turned to give her a smile, then reached up above the doorframe for the key that Detective Hendricks had told him about and held it up for her. "We are absolutely going inside. I was given permission by the police this morning."

"Seriously?" she asked, turning to him. "Wow, you do have some pull, don't you?"

"I don't, but Badger does."

"Badger?" she repeated. "Who is that?"

"He's my boss," he added helpfully.

"Oh, right, the one you're always talking to on the phone."

"Yep, that's him, and his wife makes my prosthetics. She's a hell of a designer," he added warmly.

"Wow, that field would be something I would absolutely love to get into, but I wouldn't have the first idea how."

"In her case, I think she came by it naturally because she's missing a leg herself."

"What? It's not all that common to have two of you with prosthetics."

"Oh, she deals with lots of us. Badger has a missing leg too and God-only-knows what else," he said with a smile. "They're a well-matched pair in so many ways."

"That's good," she replied. "I think people with disabilities get the short end of the stick most of the time."

"Unless they're like my brother, and they reach out and grab what they want." He turned and cast her a sideways glance. "Did I tell you he's got a girlfriend?"

She stared at him in delight. "Yep, you did, but I'm bummed that he didn't tell me himself. We see each other in passing periodically."

"He's probably afraid you'll tease him."

"Oh, I would have," she agreed, "but it would have been all in good fun. I'm absolutely thrilled for him, and it would take a special girl."

"Absolutely. It takes a special girl, but he is a very special young man," he noted warmly.

"Could you possibly be any prouder of him? It's clear that you love him more than ever."

"Oh, yes, he's not just my brother but my best friend. We've been through a lot together. That creates a very special bond, no matter what the blood relationship is."

"I never had any siblings," she murmured. "I often wondered how my life would have been different if I had had a brother or a sister."

"It's hard to say, especially with that mother of yours. It may be for the best that nobody else suffered the pain."

"I know, and I think of that sometimes. Yet I was left to endure it all alone, and that wasn't the easiest either."

"Of course not." He nodded, turning to her. "Shall we go in?" He unlocked the door and pushed it open.

They stepped inside, and she wrinkled up her nose immediately. "It's really stale smelling, isn't it?"

"Of course. Nobody is here to freshen it up and to air it out," he noted. "Unfortunately nobody has come through to confirm no break-ins, vandalism, or other trouble has been going on either."

It was like walking through a mausoleum. All the furniture was here, and still some canned goods remained in the cupboards. She sighed, the sadness creeping through her tone. "It's as if a life has been interrupted."

"More than interrupted," he clarified. "It's a life that's been put on life support. This should be all Brian's, but, until I get through to the lawyer handling the estate, I won't know for sure."

"Who will tell you that?"

"The detective assigned to the murder investigation should know, so I just need to call him."

"I highly doubt he would tell you."

"You would be surprised. If it's pertinent to their case, or pertinent to mine, generally people work together."

"Sure, but you're talking about two completely different cases."

HE NODDED AND didn't say anything. They wandered through the lower part of the house and then upstairs.

When they stopped at a huge dog bed at the top of the stairs, Risa sighed. "This just breaks my heart."

She pushed open the door and there, inside the child's room, was another large dog bed. "Well, we know where Scotty stayed."

"Yes, the two were quite bonded," Cage agreed, struggling to keep the sadness out of his own words. "Sometimes there are just no good answers, not for anyone." She winced at that. They kept walking through to the master bedroom. He frowned, as he looked around. "According to the police they didn't find anything in here that would give them any clue as to what happened to the parents."

"You don't believe that though, do you?"

"Let's just say that, until I take a look myself, I won't believe it."

"But, if they weren't wealthy, weren't involved in drugs or anything illegal, which I guess nobody really knows," she suggested, "there wasn't really any reason to kill them."

"People kill for all kinds of reasons," Cage pointed out, "and not the least of which is money, power, and hate, which is the flip side of love."

"I don't know about a *flip* side," she muttered. "It sounds as if a *sick* side to me."

He chuckled. "That's definitely one of the ways to look at it." He walked over to the night table, took a quick look in the drawer, but not a whole lot was there. He lifted up the pillows and then on an impulse—while Risa rifled through the closets, still full of clothes—he lifted up the mattress so he could see underneath. He called her over. "Can you reach that?"

Something was taped underneath the mattress. She bent down, pulled it loose, and handed it to him. "What do you think it is?" she asked.

"I don't know, but let's find out right now."

He quickly opened the envelope and inside were legal documents. He quickly shoved them back into the envelope and put them into his pocket. "That'll be something for the police and the lawyer to sort out," he stated, as he glanced around. "Did you see anything else?"

She shook her head, glancing nervously around. "No. Now that you've found that, I feel as if we need to leave."

He nodded, but there was an absentmindedness to it. "I agree, but that's a completely separate issue, as opposed to finding Scotty." And, with that, he stepped out onto the balcony and looked around the neighborhood, once again hearing a dog barking in the distance.

Risa heard it too. "It's good that people have dogs, but it's very distracting when you're looking for one in particular."

"It is," he muttered, "but …" He moved back to the little boy's room. It didn't have a balcony, but it did have a large window. He stepped up to the window and looked out. "Ah, now that makes sense. Come on. We have a dog to go meet."

"What are you talking about?" she asked, as she tried to keep up with him.

He laughed. "You'll see in a minute." And, with that, he raced outside.

CHAPTER 7

RISA FOLLOWED CAGE out of the house, wondering at his sudden surge of excitement. "What did you find? What did you see?"

He just waved her on to follow him. She kept close watch as they went into the backyard. He looked over the six-foot-tall wooden fence. "Come on. We've got to go around." So he headed back out to the front yard, then locked up the house, and walked around the block. She kept up, but he was moving at a fast clip.

"Well, I'm glad to know that the sore leg doesn't slow you down," Risa quipped.

"Nope, it sure doesn't," he confirmed cheerfully.

"I gather you have something good in your world that's making you this happy?" she asked, trying to catch up behind him.

"Absolutely I do, but I've got to be sure first."

"You think you've found the War Dog?" she asked, still puzzled.

At that, he walked around the corner and stood before a house, assessed it for a moment and then nodded. He walked up to the front door and knocked, but he got no answer. "Of course there's no answer," he muttered. "That would be way too easy."

She wasn't sure what he was going on about, but he

seemed pretty sure about something. "You could fill me in, you know?"

"I could," he replied, "but, for the moment, until we know for sure, no answer is probably the best answer." He knocked again several times, and, when he still got no answer, he walked down the sidewalk to the nearest neighbor.

When a woman opened the door and frowned at him, he smiled and began, "I was looking for your neighbor next door."

"Well, if you came for him, you might as well get that damn dog. He never stops barking."

"I might do something about that," Cage offered. "Do you know how they got the dog?"

"No, I don't, but, if you're here about a noise complaint, I've posted my own many, … many times. I am sick and tired of him."

"Does the dog ever go inside?"

"I don't know," she replied irritably. "If that's the only reason you're here …"

"Considering that I'm also trying to help your problem," Cage interrupted, "a little cooperation would be appreciated."

She groaned. "Fine. I don't know. I've talked to the cops about it, and it's just one old guy next door, and he keeps saying how the dog deserves special treatment."

"Does he give it special treatment?"

"I don't think so," she said. "I mean, he's pretty close to having to go into a home himself, and he's not quite all there, if you know what I mean."

"I presume he's been here a long time?"

"Oh God, yes, ever since I have been here, probably a lot

longer than that," she shared. "I mean, he's a fine old man, don't get me wrong, but ever since he got that dog ..."

"He doesn't keep it inside at all?"

"I told you already that I don't know. It just seems as if the dog barks constantly. The old man's also three-quarters deaf, so he doesn't care."

"Ah, so that would explain it."

"Yeah, it does, but it doesn't help the rest of us."

"Has anybody else voiced any noise complaints?"

She shook her head. "How am I supposed to know?" she said, staring at him. "You do ask the darndest questions. Feel free to go poll all the neighbors," she suggested bitterly, "because I sure don't know the answer." As she went to close the door, she added, through gritted teeth, "But if you can do something about the barking, that would be great."

As she went to close it again, Cage said, "One last question."

"What?" she snapped.

"You know the family around the corner who died?"

"Yeah, what about them? The only good thing in that family was the kid, and he was in a wheelchair. So I always thought maybe it would have been better if he'd died."

Risa couldn't believe what she was hearing. "What was wrong with the parents?" she asked, curiously unable to help herself.

The woman looked at her briefly, then dismissed her and returned her attention to Cage. It was such a rude thing, yet the woman did it almost unconsciously. "It's not as if they were rude or anything, and I'm not out there being friendly myself either, but they just seemed as if they were always hidden away."

"What do you mean?" Cage asked.

"I mean, if you walked past them, they wouldn't say hi. If you greeted them first, they would just look at you as if you were from Mars or something." She shook her head. "I probably shouldn't say anything about the dead, but they were definitely weird. Maybe the fact that they were immigrants had something to do with it."

"In what way?" Cage pressed her.

"I don't know," she stated, raising both hands. "They were just … odd, kept to themselves. I don't know if the father worked or not. It seemed as if they were always home."

"So maybe he worked from home," Risa suggested.

The neighbor woman sighed. "They have a really nice house, and he always took care of it. The guy was out mowing the lawn all the time. It's not as if they did anything wrong," she said. "I don't think that. It's just they were very private."

"Right." Cage nodded. "Good to know."

"How is the little boy? Do you know?"

"I spoke to him yesterday," Cage replied with a smile, turning to look back at her. "He's adjusting, but it's a hardship for him. Brian has lost his parents and his dog."

"Well, give him that barking dog," the lady suggested, with a nod to her neighbor. "That would suit me to a tee."

"Brian's in a foster home now," Cage shared, "and they won't take a dog."

"Of course not," the woman muttered, "but I would take a kid over a dog any day." With that, she stepped back and shut the door in their face.

As Risa walked down the steps beside Cage, she asked, "There really are people in this world like that woman, *huh?*"

"She was just being herself," Cage stated in a mild tone.

"Not like you, but she is definitely her own person."

"God," Risa muttered. "I can't imagine dealing with her day in and day out. Do you really think Brian's parents were immigrants?"

"No, but to that lady, immigrants could have been literally anybody who hasn't spent the last thirty years here," he explained. "People have strange opinions about newcomers, and sometimes you're a newcomer forever if you weren't born here."

"Right," Risa agreed. "My mother is like that too."

"She is, indeed," Cage confirmed with a smile, as he looked over at her. "Yet it's fine. Now at least we know why we're not getting an answer at the door."

"Oh, right, he's deaf."

"Exactly." Cage walked back over to the house and this time hit the doorbell several times, hoping to jar whoever was in there out of the house.

Almost instantly the door opened, and a man peered out, staring at them with a puzzled frown.

Cage smiled at him. "Hey, I'm Cage Shelton, and this is my friend Risa. I'm here regarding your dog."

Immediately he stiffened. "Oh, so you've been talking to that nosy neighbor, *huh*?"

"No, it's something completely different. I'm from the War Department." He pulled out the card that Badger had made up for him before he left.

The man looked at it, and almost immediately he seemed to stand at attention. "What can I do for you then?"

"A War Dog went missing from around here a month or so back, and we were hoping you might have seen it, heard it, or maybe even helped it," he began.

That's when Risa realized that Cage really did think the

War Dog he was looking for was the one in this man's backyard.

"I understand you have a new dog here."

"Yeah, I do. I call him Bull," he muttered. "I don't know where he came from. He just showed up one day, and he looked to be in need, and I used to work with dogs like this years ago. They're well trained, and I know a trained one when I see it. I gave him a home, but … I don't know if I can keep him for long. So I've been worrying about it lately."

"Okay, do you mind if I come meet him?"

"Sure. Do you know for sure whether it's him or not?"

"I don't know that yet, but I can certainly get his chip checked out."

"Has he got a chip?" the old guy asked.

"He should have," Cage replied. "I also have a photo of the particular dog we've been looking for."

"Any idea what happened that he would have ended up here?" He seemed to be sincerely concerned about the dog and its fate.

"Yeah, at least I think I have a pretty good idea, but it's a sad story."

"Come on in. … I am Killian Moore by the way. You can call me Killian."

With that, Cage relayed what happened to the little boy and his family. Killian started to cluck away, as if an old mother hen. "Oh my, the poor little guy. He's a lucky boy to have a War Dog as his best buddy. Every boy needs to have a dog," Killian declared, as he shook his head, "and this would have been a heck of a dog for him."

"Exactly. So, Brian's devastated now and is worried about what happened to his friend. He can't search for him, but he's been really worried about him."

"Of course. Let's go meet him." He stepped out into the backyard and at the top of his voice yelled out for Bull.

The dog was already racing toward them, and it was obvious that not only was the old man hard of hearing but he was mostly blind too because, until the dog was right there upon him, Killian didn't seem to register Bull's presence. "There he is." Killian grinned with affection as he bent down and gave Bull a greeting. "Do you think this is him?"

Cage bent down and greeted the dog, who came to him with absolutely no hesitation. Cage checked him over. "I have to scan him to see if the chip is in there," he murmured, "and I don't know if that's something I can do from here or not."

"Well, he doesn't take very kindly to car rides," Killian shared, "not that I drive anymore, but I got that impression because, anytime a vehicle comes up, he tends to run away."

"I think he was taken away by animal control when Brian, the little boy, was removed from his home as well," Cage explained. "So, I'm sure, in his mind, he associates the car ride with losing everything."

"Well, Bull's a good boy," the old man stated. "I want to confirm he'll be doing okay wherever he goes. I'll miss him, but I'm not long for this world and getting him settled is more important."

Risa smiled at him. "You seem to be doing just fine."

"Ah, but I've had my day. I'm ninety-six and still living on my own, but you know how it is. Any day I could just not wake up. It's kept me alive some just knowing there wouldn't be anyone to help Bull. I reached out to a couple places, a couple shelters, but they all seemed to be full and said they don't have room to take any more. I was worried he would be misunderstood and put down, so, in a way, you're a godsend," he shared, looking over at Cage. "The fact that the War Department is involved. ... Well, that does my heart some good."

After a few more minutes of talking to Killian, Cage asked him, "Are you okay if I leave him here with you for the time being, until I can get it sorted out?"

The old man's eyes brightened, and he smiled. "I would like that. He's been really good company." He reached down and gently scratched the dog on the back of his head. "But I would really like to see that little boy get this dog back."

"I'm afraid that's not likely right now," Cage replied. "His foster parents don't particularly want to take on a dog *and* a disabled boy."

Killian's face pinched. "Just because we live a good life doesn't mean that we end up getting good back," he muttered, as he shook his head. "I always held out hope that, ... that it worked that way. However, the older I get, the harder it is to believe it. It's a sad world out there nowadays."

As Cage and Risa walked away, Cage felt his heart tug for the old man. It seemed as if the world was full of people who just needed friends.

"I don't know how you do it," she whispered in a low tone, as they walked away. "I just want to pick up Killian and the dog, go get the boy, and settle everybody back home."

Cage chuckled. "Wouldn't it be nice if we could do that? Maybe you'll get the money for a house after all, now that your stepfather's involved. Then just think how you could do something like that."

"God, it just breaks my heart. Killian's old and yet so concerned about Scotty being taken care of, when Killian's the one who's barely surviving."

"I think he's hanging on for the dog," Cage pointed out, "and that's another reason to find a solution for this."

"When we can't help everybody," she whispered, "it just hurts." Once they'd gotten into Cage's vehicle, she stared back at the house. "Just like that, though, you found Scotty."

"Yeah. Sometimes the easiest answer is the right one."

"How was that an easy answer?" she asked, looking at him.

"The dog came home or maybe didn't really go anywhere. He may have directly gone to his friendly neighbor where Scotty could stay close but keep an eye on the house in case Brian came home," Cage suggested. "Dogs are loyal, sometimes so loyal it doesn't do them any good, and it's hard, … it's really hard on them. In this case, he obviously has a bond with that little boy."

"At least now you can tell the boy all about it."

"That's the plan, and I'm hoping that maybe we can reunite them … at least temporarily."

"Would that be a kindness though?"

"I know. I've been tossing that one around," he acknowledged. "Sometimes a kindness doesn't end up being a kindness if it just tears people even further apart."

"And yet Brian really wants to know that Scotty is safe."

"Sure, but leaving him again could be pretty rough. I don't know that his foster parents will be too interested in it."

"You really didn't like them much, did you?"

"It's not as if I have any reason *not* to like them," he replied, "and I feel bad for judging them for it from first glance. I really suspect she's in this position because they have to be."

"What do you mean by that?"

"I think that something has probably gone on in their world, and, for whatever reason, they find themselves short on funds, and this is a way to maintain face and to still look good."

"Ouch," she muttered. "You think they're more concerned about looking good?"

"Again that's a judgment on my part," Cage admitted. "I don't know whether they're more concerned about looking good or about putting food on the table. It's quite possible that their circumstances have changed, and I'm just being unkind."

She smiled and patted his arm as they walked. "Well, you weren't ever unkind for no reason, and even now you're trying to figure out how to make that old man's life a little bit better."

"Well, he's a vet," he stated, twisting to look down at her. "I don't want to be him when I hit that stage in life, with nobody to give a crap, all alone. He should be well taken care of, but I'm not sure that he is."

"Or he's just refused anything that was offered out of sheer stubbornness."

He burst out laughing at that. "You could be right. Killian did look as if he had a whole lot of attitude."

"At least at one time he did, but maybe, with time, that's something that needs to change in his world too."

"Well, he could have a few more years in him. It's hard to say, but we need to know that he'll be okay."

"You left him your card?"

"Sure, and if there's anything I can do to help, I will. I'll also call Badger and see if he can do anything for him."

"How does Badger handle it when all his guys bring home bleeding-heart cases?"

"I don't know," Cage replied. "I never had to ask. Yet, if I feel I need to, I'll do it no matter what."

"Good. Somebody needs to help protect these guys, and I really liked Killian."

"I'm sure he's a character in his own way and no doubt has been raising Cain for a lot of years," Cage said, with a smile. "Yet the world becomes much less than friendly, especially when you're single, and a senior, and in his case, a *very senior* senior," Cage noted, with a smile. "I would like to think somebody could do something for Killian."

"What does he even need is the next question," Risa said. "I don't think he will take kindly to anything that smacks of charity."

"Maybe not," Cage agreed, thinking about it, "but that doesn't mean there aren't other things that can be done. A little friendship goes a long way."

She gave a happy sigh, then slipped her hand into his. "That's right, and you're really one of the good guys, aren't you?"

He squeezed her fingers and sighed. "When you've seen what I've seen, it's easier to be nice than it is to be cruel." He shook his head. "Enough cruelty is out there already. Enough violence and mindless killing too, all in the name of God-only-knows what," he muttered. "It doesn't take a whole lot to just be a decent human being."

As they got into the vehicle, he glanced back at the house and smiled. Killian stood on his deck, hanging on to Scotty, who even now was excitedly bouncing up and down beside him.

Risa noted, "It's as if Scotty wants to come with you."

"He probably does, but I think he's also concerned about the old man," Cage added, "because that's also part and parcel of where the dog's loyalty will now lay. Somebody helped him, and I can't imagine he'll let that bond go either."

"Are dogs really that easily bonded?"

"No, but you could see how he looked at the old man, knowing that he didn't have much time and that he was quite on the delicate side."

"Right," she agreed. "Tough times for everybody."

"Sometimes it's just that way," he muttered, with a nod.

"Now where?" she asked, as they sat in the vehicle.

"Well, that's a good question. We found Scotty."

"Oh"—she stopped to stare at him—"does that mean you're leaving?"

"No, I'm not leaving yet because now I have to figure out how and what to do with the various people involved."

"Yet that's not part of your job, is it?"

He gave her half a smile and shrugged. "A job is a job. It's what you make it, and I have decided that I'll have to do more in this case."

"Okay, and what is it that you'll do?"

"I'm not completely sure yet," he shared. "I'll contact the lawyer to confirm that Brian is well taken care of. There is a mess of legal documents I need to hand over too. I'll see what the future of that house is and who, if anyone, is interested in owning it. … If it's a family member, that will require a visit to see why that family member isn't taking care of the boy."

"Probably because they can't," she pointed out. "For all you know they're also on wheels."

"Maybe," Cage replied, "but it's time for me to figure it out. I have a meeting with Brian's aunt this morning." He glanced at his watch and added, "Actually in about twenty-five minutes. Do you want to come with me, or do you want to go back home and take care of something?" He gave a vague wave of his hand, and she laughed.

"You mean, something like what, laundry?"

"Sure, if that's what you want to do this morning, you're more than welcome to."

"God no," she muttered. "I have more than enough to do in my world without that kind of crap."

"Good enough. In that case, let's head down and meet with Brian's Aunt Portia."

By the time they were on the road for ten minutes, Cage had run through all kinds of possible scenarios as to why she hadn't taken on the boy. However, by the time he got up to the house and saw the disrepair, the sagging roof, and the lopsided railing, he sighed. "Looks to be another house in bad need of care," he muttered.

"There could be a lot of reasons for that too."

As they walked up, the front door opened, and an older woman with a cane, possibly in her sixties, stared at them. "You're the one who wanted to talk to me?" she asked them.

He nodded and held out his hand. "Yes, I'm Cage Shelton. And this is my friend Risa. I'm the one who came here looking for the War Dog that Brian adopted and checking up on the family."

"Well, the family is dead," she snapped, but it was obvious that it wasn't out of coldness but pain.

"Yes." Cage nodded. "So I understand."

"Come in, come in, come in," she muttered, closing the door behind them. She shivered as she sat down, and pulled a blanket over her lap. "Now, what is it you wanted to know?"

"What happened to the family, for a start."

"They were killed in a car accident," she stated.

He nodded. "I understand there are a few more details to it than that."

Her gaze shifted to the nearby window. "I don't know whether there were or not," she began, "but I'll go to my grave wondering if I missed helping her when she needed it most."

"Maybe you should tell us exactly what happened, and then we can see how this played out."

She shrugged. "I got a phone call from Fiona, … my sister. They were on the way home from an evening out, something they rarely did. Oliver was just not into those things. Fiona even seemed to be in a good mood, thinking for the first time in a long time that maybe they would finally be okay. They'd had money problems since forever. Oliver had trouble with jobs. He got jobs, then lost them, and never seemed to hold a job for any length of time. Believe me that it was always a problem. She worked and he worked, but it seemed as if they were just on this constant collision course with fate. A company would hire her, but he would get laid off. Then, as soon as he found a job, she would get her hours cut. It was always something."

"I get how that can be a struggle." Cage nodded.

"Yeah, a constant struggle. That is the perfect way to describe it. It had been one thing after another for a very long time. Then suddenly she seemed to be really happy because they found something, … and they finally had a solution. In fact, she told me that they finally had enough money to do a few things and would take Brian to Disneyland for a holiday, their first holiday ever. I know Fiona was super excited about it. She called me from the car on their way home. Normally she wouldn't call me unless she was completely alone. She suffered so much over the ups and downs of her life that she tried to keep all the phone calls away from her husband, knowing that she was essentially bitching about how he couldn't seem to keep a job."

Portia sighed, patted her lap a couple times, and an old cat, almost as fluffy and unkempt looking as Portia was, hopped up, kneaded the surface a bit, then curled up in her lap. Her face softened as she gently stroked the old cat. "When this guy goes, I won't have anything to keep me here anymore."

"What about your nephew?" Cage asked.

She sighed heavily. "If I had the means to keep him, that would be something I would consider," she shared, "but I don't. I don't even have the physical health to get up and down the stairs on my own. I'm a lot older than my sister; seventeen years to be exact," she stated, with a smile. "She was the light of our lives, always with such a bright laugh and such a happy-go-lucky person, but she fell in love with somebody who was in and out of trouble all the time."

"What kind of trouble?" he asked.

She looked at him and shook her head. "The worst kind, and no matter what we did to convince Fiona that someone better for her was out there, she wasn't having it. And it's not as if he ran drugs or anything, but he was just lazy. … He couldn't seem to hold a job. He would get into fights and cause all kinds of trouble, which got him laid off real fast."

"Was he the instigator?" Cage asked.

"I don't even know all of it because I wasn't privy to a good share of it. Oliver didn't like it when Fiona told me about their troubles, and I don't blame him. Nobody likes to hear about the hardships that you're going through, particularly if they don't reflect well on you. So I was kept out of the loop for the most part, but I know that Fiona suffered in many ways. No matter what they did, they seemed to always end up at the bottom."

Cage let her continue because she seemed to be in a zone.

"Then something happened, and Fiona didn't really tell me much about it, just that their fortune had changed, and she thought they would be out of the worst of it. I asked her what she was talking about, but she just smiled and said that sometimes God worked in mysterious ways. They'd found something that was worth a lot of money. They were hoping to sell it, pay off their mortgage, and be okay for a while."

"Did she say what it was or where she found it?" Cage asked, keeping the sharpness out of his tone.

"Just something about their backyard, which didn't make any sense to me, but she's made all kinds of foolish statements over the years that I haven't really been able to trust. They say love is blind, and I believe it. I never did marry, so I never had that particular affliction," she quipped, with half a smile in their direction. "In Fiona's case she had it bad, and we all knew that she was saying whatever she was saying out of love, so there wasn't a whole lot we could do about it."

"Did she say how much money she would get for whatever they found?"

"Portia shook her head. "Just that it would be enough to pay off the house and would put them on easy street for a while. I did tell her that, no matter what she was doing, she needed to be sensible with the money and confirm they paid off all the bills and then put away some money for Brian. She said that, of course, they would and that she wouldn't be foolish. This was the chance of a lifetime. They just had to find somebody who would buy it."

"Well, that sounds ominous."

"I know," Portia agreed, "and I've thought about it time and time again since they died."

"Did she say anything during that drive home?"

"Yes, and I told the police that they might have had somebody following them. Fiona didn't seem too worried, was treating it like a joke, but obviously it wasn't."

"No, I don't think it was a joke at all," Cage confirmed. "The question is, did people know about this item she supposedly found, and was it theirs, or was it something that somebody else had accidentally put in the wrong yard or was lost or something?"

Portia nodded. "I thought of that too. … Believe me that I've been thinking about all of that, wondering if I could have done something," she muttered. "Or maybe I could have cautioned her about something. But she didn't even tell me how much it was worth, whether five thousand or fifty thousand, but, in her mind, fifty thousand would have been an absolute fortune. For most of us, we understand mortgages and the cost of living, and, while fifty thousand is a really nice amount, it won't put anybody on easy street."

He agreed with that. He talked with her for a few more minutes and then asked, "What about the dog, Scotty?"

"Right, the dog." She sighed. "They took it to a shelter, and I was hoping that, because it was such a special dog, it would get adopted again, assuming that part was even true," she noted, with one eyebrow raised, as she looked over at him.

"The shelter lost the dog," he noted.

She stared at him, then shook her head. "Doesn't that beat all?"

"They lost it, and the War Dog went back to the same neighborhood, ending up in the backyard of one of the neighbors."

"Good God," she muttered, "that's a lot of backyard activity."

As he thought about it, he agreed. "Did you know any of the neighbors?"

"No, not at all." Portia shook her head. "I wasn't really invited over much. They got a really good deal on the house, and they've only owned it for a little while."

"Do you think there's any chance she found the item in the house, and maybe it was something the previous owner was coming back for?"

She stared at him. "Maybe. … I never thought of that, but anything is possible. The trouble is, there's no way to find out for sure, and Oliver was just the kind of guy that, if he found it, he would never give it back. If there was an argument over ownership, he would say it was his and be pretty stubborn about it."

"Is that what you think happened?"

"She did say …"

"Now hang on, did she say *backyard*?"

"I thought it was backyard, but who knows? Maybe it was the attic." She sighed. "Fiona didn't give me much information, and I didn't think to ask because she wasn't making a whole lot of sense, and she was half giddy."

"Had she been drinking?"

Portia nodded. "Maybe a little bit, but she wasn't a drinker. So I presume it was a celebratory drink. I don't even know what to tell you."

"That's fine. I'll follow up with the police."

"Good, because, if they were murdered, I would very much like to see that person brought to justice."

Cage asked, "And all those neighbors, they didn't have anything to do with Fiona?"

"I spoke to one neighbor who told me how Brian was such a lovely child. And he is," she agreed, with a nod. "Everybody loved him. What a shame he was born with spina bifida and has been in a wheelchair for his whole life. Those medical expenses were a big hit to their finances too."

"Would Oliver have gotten into anything shady in order to get them out of this financial hole they were in?"

"Oh, absolutely," she agreed. "I told the cops that too because, in the back of my mind, I always thought that maybe he was involved in something and got run off the road for it."

"Maybe so," Cage acknowledged. "I don't know what the house looked like before, but I went inside, and nothing appears to stand out as different or moved or ransacked. The home did appear to be completely normal."

"Fiona was a spotless housekeeper," Portia admitted. "She always felt good about how she could always keep the house clean. Of course she didn't have a child running around destroying it, and anything Brian did run into, he did it on wheels. So that was a completely different story."

"How long had they been in the house?"

"Less than a year, and they were still sorting through a bunch of the old stuff left in the attic and the garage. Oh, good God," she muttered, "I bet you that's where it was."

"What?"

"There had been a fight initially about who owned the

items left behind, but, because they bought the house as-is, with all that there when they moved in, it was deemed to be basically theirs. Fiona was still sorting through the stuff. Since they didn't have a lot of money, she was looking to see if she could sell any of it."

"So, you're thinking that's where she found the item."

"But why would she say *backyard* and not tell me it was up in the attic or down in the garage?"

"Hard to say," Cage replied. "Maybe some of it had been taken out to the garage and put in a pile in the backyard to take to charity or to the garbage or to set up a yard sale or whatever."

"That could be it too because Oliver wasn't very good at such things. He would have just pointed Fiona to it all and told her, *If you think you can sell it, you sell it.*"

"Interesting," he murmured.

"I know I'm not speaking well of him, and I don't mean to besmirch someone who's dead and can't defend himself, but he really wasn't the kind of person who you want to see your family member marry. He was just really flaky," she added.

Cage nodded. "It helps us to understand what may have been going on in Fiona's life."

"The question is whether any of this had to do with their deaths."

"Do you know who inherits the house?"

Portia shook her head. "I asked the police about it, and the cop said it would be part of the will, but he didn't have details. I phoned a couple of local lawyers, but nobody is saying anything as to who's looking after the will. If I'm not mentioned in it, then I guess they won't contact me. Why would they?" She shrugged. "So I really don't know."

"Do you know anything about Oliver's lawyer?"

"Last I heard we had the same lawyer," she stated, "but he didn't tell me anything when I called him recently."

"Well, if he didn't, then by law he's probably not allowed to."

"*Hmm.*" She frowned at him. "What about you? Can you find out that information?"

"I'll see. If I do, I'll let you know."

"It should go to Brian," Portia declared. "God knows he'll need it."

He smiled and nodded. "He absolutely will. I was hoping you were in a position to take him in, and Scotty too."

"God no," she muttered with a sigh. "I'm barely able to stay out of a home myself, and that's not where I want to spend the rest of my life," she muttered. "Those places are terrible."

"Some of them are good," he clarified, "but you do have to look for one."

"Well, if you ever find a good one, then let me know," she said, with a cackle, "because it sure seems as if they're all out for money and not very much for helping the very people they are there to care for."

They spoke for a few minutes longer, and then Cage stood up. Risa followed suit. Portia walked them to the door and added, "Remember what you told me though. If you find out anything, let me know."

"Will do," Cage confirmed, as they stepped out into the fading sunshine.

"How did the weather turn so quickly?" Risa asked at his side. "It was beautiful when we went in."

"Yeah, but these subject matters tend to throw a pall over it too, doesn't it?"

"God, does it ever stop? It seems as if we're just finding one sad case after another."

"Poverty can do that," he noted, shaking his head.

"And Portia's living in a pretty run-down house. If she had any money coming to her, it could go a long way, but wouldn't the lawyer have contacted her already?"

Cage shrugged. "If I were to guess, it depends. The attorney might not settle anything until they sort out cause of death. If there was any suspicion that the couple were murdered, I imagine the attorney would have to hold off on settling the estate for a while. However, I don't know how that works."

"Interesting," she muttered. "I guess it's easier to hold back than to claw back."

"Exactly, and that's our next stop."

"Have you already contacted the lawyer?"

He nodded. "I did, and now it's time for a more in-depth conversation."

"Good enough," she muttered, but she hesitated.

He suggested, "I could drop you off, if you like."

"If you wouldn't mind that. Even though I would love to hear what the lawyer has to say, … I'm not sure it's my forte."

"No, it's probably better if you aren't there for this one," he agreed, with a reassuring smile. "I'll fill you in afterward."

"You could always come to my place for dinner," she offered impulsively.

He smiled at her and nodded. "That's a great idea." Minutes later, he pulled up to her place, and she waved him off, then turned and headed inside.

CAGE DROVE OVER to the lawyer's office, and, just as he walked up, a man stepped out and turned to lock up the doors. "Excuse me," Cage said. Startled, the man turned, looked at him. "Sorry to catch you on your way out, but I called you earlier."

"Oh, you must be Cage Shelton."

"Yes, and you must be Mr. Xavier. I was hoping we could talk for a minute."

"I really can't give you any confidential information."

"I'm aware of that," Cage noted, "but I'm also aware that, as far as the police were concerned, foul play may have been involved in the parents' deaths."

Xavier nodded solemnly. "That's the indication, and that just makes my job all that much harder," he shared cautiously.

"I'm sure that the will is pretty simple though, since Brian and Portia are the only family that I know of. In this case, as I'm sure you are aware, the boy is the one we're all concerned about."

"Of course, of course," Xavier replied, "and everything is taken care of, but the boy is in foster care at the moment."

"Yes, and we're wondering if there isn't something that can be done about that."

"I don't see how," he stated, frowning at him. "I mean, that's what foster care is for."

"*Right*," Cage conceded, with a dry smile. "Putting kids with disabilities in homes where they're not really wanted."

"Oh dear." Xavier looked horrified. "Is it that bad?"

"Well, it's not great," Cage stated. "Only a few people out of the masses are truly equipped to handle a disabled child such as Brian, but, because they pay extra money for these foster cases, lots of people sign up, and they probably shouldn't have."

"Oh," Xavier muttered and pinched the bridge of his nose. "I was really hoping that Brian was doing okay."

"And I'm really hoping that the estate has been settled properly and that Brian will be okay when he turns eighteen, if nothing can be done in the meantime."

Xavier stared at him. "Well, I hope you're not thinking I'm doing anything illegal?"

"I would hope not," Cage responded, "because that would just piss me off and that won't do any of us any good."

Xavier stiffened. "You know that I don't have to talk to you."

"Nope, you don't," Cage agreed, "but, considering you're the one privy to the information and the police have been around to talk to you, I need your cooperation."

"Sure, but only because of the pending murder case," the lawyer acknowledged, "and I am cooperating with the detective on the case. Hendricks just wanted to know who would inherit, and I was legally bound to tell him. Now it's their issue to confirm that whoever killed Brian's parents doesn't get the money."

"I don't think that'll be an issue in this case," Cage replied.

Xavier hesitated and eyed him cautiously. "Everything is in order. I'm just waiting for the police to close the file."

"What if they don't?"

He shrugged. "I have a certain number of days until I have to close it anyway."

"Who'll handle the child's money after this?"

"I can appoint a trustee, and I guess I could probably deal with some of that myself," he shared, pondering it for a moment. "It's something that I wish his parents had set up with some clear instructions, but nobody ever thinks it'll be their time and that they won't be around forever."

"Of course, and yet it never is that way, is it?"

"No, unfortunately it's not."

Cage knew it was unfair, but it was part and parcel of life. Cage added, "In regard to Brian, he should be fine, but if he can't have access to his money until he's eighteen, we must confirm that whoever looks after it is trustworthy. If some family member wanted to care for Brian in the family home, then I would presume that Brian has almost immediate access to that asset." Cage shook his head. "I sure don't want that young boy, who has already suffered so much, to suffer more when he comes of age and finds out that somebody has squandered away his money."

"Well, I won't be the trustee," Xavier noted sharply. "If you want to put forward some names of people who are trustworthy, then I'll be happy to consider them. We'll see what we can come up with."

"That I can do," Cage agreed, with a smile.

"Are you sure you're not related to the family in any way? You seem to be quite concerned." Xavier asked.

"I *am* quite concerned. I'm quite concerned about Scotty, the War Dog, who has bonded with Brian. Now, after seeing the situation the boy's in, I'm quite concerned about Brian." Cage sighed. "There's enough hardship in this world without Brian being hit with even more."

"Yeah, I won't argue that," Xavier said soberly. "So give me a name or two, and I'll consider them."

"Will do, and, if you hear anything from Detective Hendricks, or you have any other issues to deal with regarding the estate, please let me know."

The lawyer hesitated. "I'm just trying to confirm that the boy is looked after and that somebody who shouldn't have access to his money doesn't get it."

"Good." Cage nodded.

"I know that's what the police are concerned about as well, so they're looking into this just as they should, and I'm not allowed to talk about it."

"Of course you're not allowed to talk about that part," Cage noted, with a smile, "but we all know exactly how the system works. So, meanwhile we need to confirm that Brian is taken care of." And, with that, Cage turned and walked away.

Xavier called out after him, "You know that you could have just talked to the police?"

"I *did* talk to the police," Cage confirmed, turning back and catching the surprised look on the attorney's face. "However, I go the extra mile to double-check that the information is correct. So I needed to know that boy will be looked after and that nobody will try and take away his money."

Xavier nodded. "Well, you don't need to look at me," he declared in a testy voice. "I've got big-enough problems without adding more to that. I've got two ex-wives always looking for a reason to squeeze me for more, and believe me that this isn't something I'm prepared to get into trouble over."

"That also makes you a very likely person to help yourself to Brian's money," Cage pointed out, "and believe me, if I see that happening, … I would put you in jail myself."

"That's not happening," he snapped, staring at him, visibly distraught.

"So, there will be a full accounting of every penny spent,

correct?"

"Of course, of course," he stated stiffly. "Are you a law-yer?"

"No, but I have a whole team of lawyers behind me," Cage shared, with a smile, as he took several more steps to his car. "Just so you know, they'll be reviewing everything you do, so keep that in mind." Realizing that he had scared the lawyer to the point that he might be too upset to drive himself home, Cage called out with a smile. "Have a nice day." With that, he got into his vehicle and drove away.

Only as he drove down and around the block, he realized that he'd picked up a tail.

CHAPTER 8

RISA SET THE spaghetti sauce off to the side, not sure exactly when Cage would arrive but wanting to be ready just in case. When the phone rang, she winced to see it was her mother.

"What are you playing at?" Eleanor roared into the phone.

She cleared her throat loudly. "I have no clue what you're talking about, but could you turn down the volume, please?"

Eleanor cried out, "God, what is wrong with you?"

"Well, apparently you," Risa snapped right back.

"How dare you get involved in my divorce?"

"I didn't get involved in your divorce," she declared. "I don't want anything to do with it."

"And yet you spoke to Graham."

"What? I'm not allowed to speak to him now?"

Eleanor almost bellowed now. "No, you're not, and I've made that abundantly clear."

"Well, that's just too bad," Risa stated. "He invited me out for dinner, and I will most likely go. I really liked him."

"Well, … that's just stupid on your part," Eleanor claimed, "because, believe me, it'll backfire."

"In what way will it backfire?"

"I'll confirm that it does," she snapped, and then she

quickly disconnected.

What the hell was that all about?

Risa wasn't sure what was going on, but she really didn't want to get involved any more than she had to. If her mother and Graham were arguing and fighting, then it was important that Risa stayed out of it, for her own mental health if nothing else.

When the phone rang again, she noted it was her stepfather.

"I'm so sorry, honey. I know she spoke to you, didn't she?"

"Is that what it was?" Risa quipped, a note of humor in her voice. "It sounded more like a tirade."

"Yes, of course it did. I guess she received some of the paperwork today. She called me and told me that any contact with you was a complete deal breaker, so I had to tell her that I'd already had contact with you. Therefore, Eleanor couldn't have a deal breaker when it was already something in progress. I hope you won't let her stop us from seeing each other?"

"No, I wasn't planning on it," she murmured, "and her tirade just now was hot and furious."

"Yes, that's her. She's always been quite a feisty woman," he murmured, and still, admiration filled his tone.

Risa groaned. "Please tell me that you're not trying to get her back again."

"No, I'm not," he muttered. "I realized long ago that she's not one of those people I would always love to be around. She's like a fire and burns everything around her." He sighed. "I'm exhausted and really just want to have this over with in a good way."

"That would be nice," Risa agreed.

"And how about dinner next week?"

She smiled. "That would be fine."

They chose Tuesday night, and he added, "I'll come pick you up." And, with that, he disconnected.

Risa had to smile, as she realized just how pissed off her mother would be over this. Risa hadn't done this for that sole purpose by any means, but, now that it was in progress, she felt a weird sense of satisfaction in pissing off Eleanor.

Realizing that it didn't put Risa in the best light, she muttered to herself, "I don't care."

She quickly worked on making a big salad, and, when the phone rang again, she sighed. "Now who?" She picked up the phone to hear it was Cage. "Hey," she greeted him. "How long until you're in for dinner?"

"I don't know," he grumbled, his tone grim. "I've got a tail on me."

"What?" she asked, not understanding.

"Somebody is following me," he clarified.

"Oh, good God," she cried out. "What can I do? What do you want me to do?"

"Nothing. I'm just telling you that I might be a little delayed. Plus, I don't want you going anywhere. I don't know what this is about. I don't know whether it has to do with all the inquiries into the accident that killed Brian's parents, or even whatever is going on with whoever has been poking around at your place."

"Right," she muttered, "the Peeping Tom."

"Exactly, so just stay inside and keep everything locked up, okay? I'll be there as soon as I can." And, with that, he disconnected.

She absolutely hated the idea of somebody out there try-ing to run Cage off the road, just like what had happened to

Brian's parents. As she sat here worrying about him, Celine called. Realizing that it was at least a distraction, Risa answered, hoping for a light, gentle conversation, but instead Celine was crying hysterically. "Are you okay? What's going on? What's the matter, Celine?" Straightening up in her chair, she got very direct with her friend. "What happened?"

"He left," she wailed. "He left."

"Who left?"

"My boyfriend," she muttered, "the new one."

"Oh." She sat back down and rubbed her face, wondering just how many times in the last year she'd had a similar conversation with Celine. "I'm sorry if he broke up with you."

"No, you don't understand. He's *gone*, gone. He told me that he never really wanted anything to do with me and was just looking for information. Then he said he would check you out."

It was confusing, but Risa heard that last part. "What are you talking about? Come on now, Celine. This is important. What information was he looking for, and why has it got anything to do with me?"

"I don't know, but I figured that he saw you and, like everybody else in the world, preferred you."

"Good God," Risa groaned. "You know that's not true."

"It is true," Celine cried out, wailing at the top of her lungs. "Everybody always prefers you."

Risa was really not in the mood for this and yet unsure how to get more information out of her friend. Still, Risa chastised her friend. "That's not true, and you know it, but you need to tell me right now what was he looking for, what information?"

"About the house beside me. I told him that you guys

were looking into the murders."

"Why would you do that?" Risa asked.

"Well, because it's true."

"No, it's not true, and it's not something you go telling everybody, good God." She stared down at the phone, wondering if this explained some of what was going on—including Cage being followed. "You told a complete stranger that nonsense, and now somebody is following Cage, who is out on the road. Those people who were killed were on the road too," she snapped. "What the hell have you done?"

"I didn't do anything," Celine muttered, crying her eyes out. "It's not fair for you to accuse me."

"Oh, right," Risa snapped, "and here you are, babbling away, telling people that we're investigating a murder? Good God, Celine. He's looking for a lost War Dog, *not* for the murderer." Risa wanted to shake Celine, so she would wake up and realize what she'd done.

"Well, I thought you were," she muttered, crying.

"We're not. We were looking for a missing War Dog, and that's it."

"Yeah, but it's the War Dog that belonged to the family."

"Sure, a War Dog from the family, but not a dog that we're looking for because somebody was murdered, for crying out loud. We were looking for the War Dog because he was missing!"

"Well, how was I supposed to know?"

Risa snorted and shook her head. No point in talking to Celine when she was still upset and more or less pissed off because this guy had supposedly taken off after her. "At least he doesn't know where I live." At that, Celine went silent, and fear gripped her. "Oh God," Risa screamed. "You told him where I lived?"

"I didn't tell him which apartment you lived in, just the name of your building," Celine spat, clearly still angry. "I only said that you lived in the Eldorado Arms."

"Christ," she whispered, sagging down into her chair.

"What are you talking about?"

"Why would you do that, Celine?"

"I didn't think it was important."

"You pointed some guy who could be a psychopath in my direction. You may very well have told him where I live."

"But he was my boyfriend at the time," she whined, "so it's not as if I was expecting it to be an issue."

"No, no, *of course not*," Risa quipped, staring down at her phone in horror. "You do realize I've had some stalker, a Peeping Tom, staring in my window the other night."

"How the hell would I know that?" she asked. "It's not as if you told me."

"No, I didn't tell you because you were busy with your bloody new boyfriend."

"He's gone now," she snapped, "all because of you." And, with that, Celine disconnected the phone.

Now Risa was half panicked and half in disbelief. What kind of a friend would tell somebody—casually or not—that their friend lived in a specific building?

Of course, to give Celine some credit, she didn't realize that this guy might give a crap, and at that point had not given Celine any indication that he was dangerous. So from her friend's perspective, it was just a simple question. Yet, if Celine really thought of Risa as competition, what the hell was she doing talking about Risa and where she lived? She shook her head. Celine had always had a mouth on her and never could keep anything inside her head.

They'd been friends since forever, but, as Risa sat here, staring down at the phone, she realized just how far off the grid this friend of hers had gone. Nobody else in her acquaintance would have shared personal information, just from a commonsense safety perspective of a single woman living alone.

That Celine had done it was just too unbelievable. Especially since she was the one always worried about people coming into her space, and here she was blabbing all this information about Risa to some guy Celine barely knew and had been sleeping with for just a matter of a few days.

When the phone rang again, she stared down at it, loath to answer, until she recognized Cage's number. "Are you okay?" she demanded right off the bat, only to find Cage wasn't on the other end.

A sinister laugh came. "Oh, I'm okay, but I don't think your friend is." And, with that, the phone went dead.

CAGE OPENED HIS eyes slowly, trying to figure out what the hell happened. As he went to move, his leg refused to cooperate. He groaned, his head throbbing.

A man spoke nearby. "It doesn't matter what the hell you do, you're not getting loose."

Cage stiffened at that, then slowly opened his eyes again and glared at him. "What the hell happened?"

"I cut your gas line, so I knew you would run out at some point. I didn't want to give you much chance to argue, so I came up behind you, pulled open the door, and whacked you over the head. You were obviously well prepared and ready for me, but I took you out before you had a chance to even think about defending yourself. So, hey, don't worry about it. I was in the military, and it's the stuff I used to do."

It was on the tip of Cage's tongue to say he was military too, but, since he hadn't come out the winner on this one, it seemed pointless to argue. "What do you want?" Cage asked, shifting uncomfortably.

"Well, you see? That's the trouble. What I want from you is something I'm not sure you can give me."

"So why the hell am I here?" he asked in astonishment.

"In case there's any chance you know where it is."

"Any chance I know where what is? I don't even know what you're talking about."

"A diamond, a big diamond."

"And that big diamond is yours?"

"Well, it should be, as it belonged to my grandfather, who had the house before your lovely little family lived there."

"I don't even know who you are or what family you're talking about."

"The house that you were in today, and the house that you keep bugging people about, … and that family, all about this boy."

"You're talking about the boy's parents who were killed?"

"Yeah, the family I killed," he declared, sneering. "The bloody idiots found the diamond, told me all about it, and then told me that I couldn't have it because it was theirs, how they would sell it and make lots of money. I told them that I would pay for it, but they didn't seem to want to do that either. Of course they figured they could get more money elsewhere, and they probably could have. They might have been able to make lots more, except for the fact that I wouldn't let them get away with it."

"How so?"

"It was my grandfather's house, and I sold it to them. I was the fool who said everything was included, not realizing that the diamond wasn't in the safety deposit box, and I've been hunting for it ever since. Then I heard they found it in some of the boxes up in the attic. My grandfather had put it up there, probably for safekeeping, the old fool, but they wouldn't have anything to do with giving it back to me," he muttered. "So, what choice did I have?"

"So, you killed them for it?" Cage asked, frowning at him.

"Well, it sounds rough when you say it that way."

"Is there any other way to say it?" Cage asked. "I mean, you killed a family because of a diamond."

"I didn't kill a whole family," he clarified. "I just popped that asshole. The fact that he was driving at the time just made it more convenient."

"Did you shoot him?"

"No, I shot out the tires, and he ran off the road," he shared, with a smile. "So, I really didn't do anything."

"*Right*," Cage muttered, thinking about the misguided logic that this asshole was utilizing. "Now, what is it that you want from me?"

"I want that diamond."

He just stared at the man. In the darkness it was hard to even begin to see features, and that was probably deliberate. "How am I supposed to find this diamond?"

"Well, you were talking to the lawyer today."

"I was, but what does that have to do with it?"

"I'm thinking he might have it."

"I don't know anything about that," Cage replied, thinking about it. "On the other hand, if you threatened him, you might get some information." Then realized this asshole would likely do just that.

The other guy just laughed. "Oh, don't worry. I was thinking about it, but I don't want too many of these incidents cropping up in just a matter of days. Getting caught would really blow my plans out of the water."

"Presumably you just want the diamond so you can take off?"

"Yes, I want to sell it and take off," he confirmed. "That's exactly what I want to do. Why the hell would anybody hang on to a big diamond like that?"

"Why did your grandfather hang on to it?" Cage asked.

"Because he got it from a mine that he worked at a long time ago. It was a gift for his wife, my grandmother. She wouldn't wear it because it was such a valuable piece, so they just hung on to it, which was just stupid. If you've got a piece like that, you might as well wear it. There's no other point to having jewelry."

"But a lot of people don't wear jewelry when it's so expensive," he pointed out.

"And that's what I'm saying. It makes no sense. If you have a piece that's beautiful, then wear it. Otherwise it's not so beautiful and why keep it?"

"How is it I'm supposed to find the diamond in their house? It's still the same, nothing's been touched. You can go through it yourself."

"I have," he muttered in frustration. "I have."

"Did you look in the vehicle? Apparently the wife called her sister and discussed something about they would be on easy street now all because they found something in the backyard."

"Backyard?" he asked sharply.

"That's what Fiona told her sister, but then you ran them off the road. Who knows? It might have been in the vehicle."

"Well, shit," the gunman muttered. "I don't even know where the vehicle is."

"Neither do I," Cage replied in exasperation, "but probably still in the police impound, locked up as evidence of the murders."

He looked at Cage and nodded. "That's where we're going then."

"The impound lot?" Cage asked.

"Yeah. How else will I find the diamond?"

"I have no idea, but you're just as likely to find it if you go back to the house and take another look."

"We'll do that too."

"You know I have places to be and other things to do, right?" Cage asked, with a note of humor.

"Not right now, you don't," the gunman stated, his voice turning ugly. "Your whole point right now is to help me find that diamond. Otherwise I go back and find your girlfriend."

At that, Cage stiffened, and the other man nodded. "Yeah, I know about her. Somebody I just met has done nothing but talk about her ad nauseam. Jesus, it's enough to make me sick."

"Oh, I get it," Cage noted, nodding in understanding. "You're Celine's new boyfriend."

"No, I'm really not. I was Celine's quick lay," he clarified, with a snort, "but that girl just talks too damn much."

"I'm sure she'll love hearing that."

"We've already broken up, and I told her that I was coming after your girlfriend."

"Why the hell would you do that?"

"Because she told me how you were looking into this murder."

"I'm not looking into any murder," Cage replied in exasperation, but inside he was ready to punch Celine for her part in this. "I'm looking for a War Dog. I work for the War Department, and I'm just here to find a dog that went missing."

"That kid's dog?"

"Sadly, because you went and knocked off the kid's family, he couldn't have his dog back, even if I find it."

"Oh, boo-hoo. Apparently, because I popped the family, I can't get my fucking diamond back either," he snapped, "so who cares?"

"*Right*, you're just all about you."

"Help me find the diamond," he suggested, "and then you can go free."

Of course Cage knew that was a whole lot easier said than done, particularly since he could now identify the man and had heard him admit to the murders. So no way this guy would let Cage go. Cage held his thoughts because saying anything would spook this murderer.

The gunman asked, "So do you really think that it's in the car?"

"No, I don't."

"But you seem to think—"

"I'm just saying that's one more potential location. Otherwise did you check the attic where the diamond was supposedly found?"

"Yes, but I didn't find it." The gunman thought about that for a minute. "All right, let's go." Pointing to the side, he added, "We'll go in my vehicle. You can drive, and we'll go check out the attic."

"If you say so," Cage said, as he struggled to get up, groaning with pain.

"I didn't hit you that hard," the gunman muttered.

"No, but I'm an injured war vet myself," he muttered.

He snorted at that. "Ain't no good coming from serving the country. What a crock. They leave you on the side of the road like a cripple when they don't want you no more."

"Is that what they did to you?"

"Damn right that's what they did to me. I served until suddenly one day I was discharged."

"What did they say?"

"Something about unfit to serve. I don't know what the fuck they were talking about since I was plenty fit to serve when they needed somebody to hold guns and shoot, but after that? Oh no, suddenly I'm not fit to be in the military anymore." He shook his head. "I don't care. I'm tired and frustrated. I didn't want to sell the house in the first place, but I needed the money. Then, sure enough, those assholes find the goddamn diamond. But instead of just selling it and walking away, he had to call me up and let me know. What an arrogant prick."

"I haven't heard much nice about him, I have to admit."

"No, there sure as hell wasn't anything nice about that asshole, but that's the way life is, isn't it?"

Cage shrugged. "Sometimes people have all the luck, and other times it seems as if they've got luck, but they really don't because somebody takes it away from them."

At that, the gunman burst out laughing. "You got that

right." He chuckled. "I got that asshole in the end."

"That you did," Cage agreed, trying to keep his tone neutral.

He snapped, "Now come on. Let's get up."

"I'm up," Cage growled, as he strode slowly toward the other vehicle.

"You can drive, right?"

"Yeah, I can drive," he grunted, "but I don't know where we are, so you'll have to give me directions."

"Yeah, another thing," he said, holding up a hand, "no funny stuff. Once you kill the first one, every other one after that becomes that much easier. In the military, I took down plenty," he admitted, his tone turning ugly. "So don't think you'll turn on me now."

"Wasn't thinking of it," Cage muttered, keeping the fatigue in his voice. "I've got too much PTSD of my own right now to bother trying to climb into your head."

"Good, in that case, we should get along just fine."

Moving slowly, Cage headed toward the vehicle pointed out to him. Once he got there, he took several deep breaths, casually glancing around before being nudged into the driver's seat. As soon as he was in, the asshole climbed into the back seat, right behind Cage, and sat directly over his shoulder.

"You pull any funny stuff, and you know who'll get the first bullet."

"Of course," Cage noted in a calm voice. "Where to?"

"You know where to," he snapped.

Cage sighed. "Which direction from here? As I said, I don't know where we are."

With a grumble, the gunman pointed north. "We'll go look for that goddamned diamond. Do you think the car or the house though?" he asked, as he pondered over where a diamond could be. "Now that I've had a chance to think about it," he added, nudging Cage with the gun, "the house would probably be better."

"I think so too," Cage agreed. "Oliver might have been tricky, but I don't think he was terribly brilliant."

"No, he wasn't, and doing what he did confirmed that. Absolutely no way I could let him live after that, and he couldn't seem to figure that out."

"Did you talk to him before you popped him?"

"He was still alive, … after I ran him off the road. I went down to talk to him, to see if my work was done, and he kept begging for help," the gunman shared, with a sneer. "His wife was already dead, and not a whole lot I would do to help him at that point, especially when he wouldn't tell me where the goddamn diamond was."

"Well, considering he lost his life over it, I'm not surprised," Cage replied in a mild-enough tone. "Think about it. What would you do if somebody did that to you?"

"I would make sure they paid, one way or another," he claimed, his tone dark. "I would make damn sure they paid."

"Well, you made them both pay, and they didn't have any way to pay you back except to withhold information. So it looks to me as if all they did is exactly what you would have done to them."

The gunman gave a hard kick to the back of the driver's seat. "That's enough out of you," he snapped. "Now head to the house. We'll go there first."

Delighted with that option because the house gave Cage all kinds of ways to sort through this, he headed to Brian's old house, following the gunman's directions. When Cage pulled up in the front, the gunman shook his head.

"No, drive around to the back."

Pulling back into traffic, Cage headed around the corner and came up into the alleyway. "Does he have a garage back here? I never did see one."

"Yeah, there's a garage all right, but it's full of shit too."

"Well, that could be where he kept it."

"Why would you leave a diamond that's worth millions in an old garage?"

"I wouldn't," Cage stated truthfully. "Yet you've already searched the attic, so I guess that leaves the garage. I'm not sure where I would keep a big diamond. I've never had anything like that on my radar. It's an interesting question though."

"Well, it's a moot point for you because this diamond is damn special, and it's mine," he snapped.

"What about your family?"

"No family is left," he said, "so I just don't give a fuck anymore. It's one thing if you've got somebody who loves you and is there waiting for you, but, when everyone is dead and gone, you start to not give a shit anymore."

Cage could understand that, but still, he had to come up with a way to get through to this guy. "What about all those people who do have somebody who loves them, … like that couple you killed? What about the little boy?"

"Well, he drew the unlucky straw because he had assholes for parents." He spat and then motioned to Cage. "Now you'll get out, and you'll open that garage."

"Do you really think I can pull the car into it, if it's full of garbage?"

The gunman hesitated. "Shit, we'll just park here." Then he nudged him again with the gun. "No funny stuff."

Cage got out of the vehicle, and together the two of

them walked to the side door of the garage. The gunman pulled it open, keeping the gun on Cage, always wary, always alert.

It was the alertness that revealed the gunman's military background as much as anything. This guy hasn't once come down off that mountain. Cage felt sorry for him for a few minutes, then realized that this guy was too far gone.

As far as the gunman was concerned, it was him against the entire world, and nobody else out there understood. Maybe they didn't, and that was always a problem when it came to PTSD and the psychological damage that so many vets sustained while they were over there. But no matter what happened to them, it could never justify this madness.

Everybody thought about all the physical damage done to the veterans, but a massive amount of psychological damage happened to these guys that the powers that be needed to spend more time considering. They needed to come up with suitable and effective treatment, although it was hard to imagine that this guy would have pursued it anyway. "Did you ever get therapy?" Cage asked calmly, as they opened up the garage.

"What therapy would they give me? I'm discharged. … Remember?"

"Medically?"

"They gave me enough to keep my pension," he muttered, "and that's it, and it isn't a very good pension at that."

"But you should have been able to access some of the medical services, like therapy," Cage pointed out again.

"I won't talk to a shrink or let anybody inside my head," he snapped, poking Cage in the back with his gun, "and I know you wouldn't either."

"I did some therapy," Cage shared. "When you start losing limbs, the military really doesn't like it if you don't go talk to somebody. And, just so you know, talking to somebody is not the same thing as having them in your head. Sometimes therapy is helpful."

"Good. I'm happy for you," he snapped in a sarcastic tone. He turned on the lights and swore. "This is ridiculous. No way he would hide a diamond in here."

"Except for the fact that you know full well that nobody'll get through all this, so in a way it's a perfect hiding spot."

"Well, you better get at it then," he said, glaring. "You've got a lot of sorting to do."

Cage rubbed his temple as he stared at the mess. "I don't even know where to start."

"And neither do I, though I've searched everywhere around here."

"Is this your shit or theirs?"

"It's probably a combination of both," he muttered, shaking his head. "He was a bit of a hoarder."

"Who was, your dad?"

"My granddad," he corrected. "He said everything always had a use, so he never really got rid of anything, which was the problem. I could never find the damn thing and would have thought a safe deposit box made the most sense. And, for normal people, it would, … except he didn't trust banks. So that was another hurdle I had to deal with."

"You never heard about it from anybody in the family?"

"No, my grandmother told me that she had no idea where it went, and it was hers anyway. Yet, when I told her that she wouldn't live long enough to see it again, she didn't want me to have it. She gave me a look that told me that she really didn't like me. Such a bitch. Honest to God, my family has been a big disappointment."

"Did you hurt her?"

"No, I didn't have to hurt her. She was already pretty-far gone, and there wouldn't have been anything in it for me."

"And of course you only do what's good for you."

"I only do what'll give me something. As if you'd do anything else."

"Well, I would like to think I *could* do something else," Cage noted, "but I can see how that wouldn't be up your alley."

"Yeah, ya think?" he muttered. "You guys are all such bleeding hearts. But everybody's out to get you, remember? It's kill or get killed, and nothing else matters."

"That'll be a very lonely way to live when you finally get your money and take off."

"Not likely," he argued, giving him a smile. "A million girls like Celine are out there, just waiting for someone to give them some attention. I don't really give a shit about them either."

"But that's what I mean, it'll be lonely."

"No, not when you've got money. It's never lonely with money. A lot of Celines are around the world."

It was such a depressing way to think about life, but it wasn't the first time Cage had heard such a motto. "If you say so," he muttered, as he looked around the garage. "So, you tell me where you want me to start."

The gunman looked around and a hint of that angry fire filled his gaze. "Christ, I don't know. Where the hell would they keep something like that? A black leather pouch, small drawer, box inside of a box inside of a box? I don't know," he groaned, raising both hands.

"There's a lot of stuff to go through here," Cage noted.

"Well, you need to find it, because I'm not letting you go until you do."

The fact of the matter was, this guy wouldn't let Cage go no matter what, whether he found it or not. The gunman couldn't afford to, and no way he would let Cage walk out of here alive. So, it was all about getting out of here before that could happen.

Just as he started moving toward a bunch of boxes, Cage heard a dog in the distance. He hid a smile because, of course, that was Scotty, and, boy, was that a welcome sound.

"Damn dog," the gunman muttered, "that thing kicks up a fuss every time I'm in the neighborhood."

"It's just a dog," Cage pointed out. "They're meant to kick up a fuss when people are where they don't belong."

The gunman gave a snort at that. "Isn't that the truth. They're a hell of a lot smarter than people, that's for sure."

"Were you in the house a lot recently?" Cage asked.

"Every damn night it seems," the gunman replied. "I just want what's mine."

"I'm sorry. … I'm sorry that this took a turn that required people to lose their lives," Cage said, "but it wasn't necessary to destroy that little boy's family."

"Yeah, well, I'll be the judge of that," he snarled. "Remember how you don't know shit."

"No, I don't." Cage sighed, as he moved boxes around, trying to make a space to get in and to see what was here. "I still think that this would be a shitty place to keep a diamond."

"Why?" the other man asked.

"Because I wouldn't want to let it out of my sight."

"Ha. That was the premise I had when I started searching the house, but, honest to God, I didn't see it anywhere."

"What if Brian's parents already sold it?"

"I don't know. I don't know what if then," he muttered. "I mean, in that case I'm screwed."

"You don't have enough money to live on?"

"Nope, and they're stopping my benefits apparently."

"Well, you can probably get that reviewed."

"Sure, I get there and fight for another few dollars, a few dollars that I earned the hard way," he snapped. "It's not fair."

"No, I'm sure it's not," he muttered. "I haven't come up against that yet."

"Well, you will because, one way or another, they'll make damn sure that you don't get whatever it is that you think you've got coming."

Cage didn't say anything, but it wasn't the first time he'd heard people bitch about their VA benefits. He wasn't sure exactly what it would look like for him, as he'd just now completed surgery and rehab. He knew he had some review to go through later, to see whether he was capable or not, to determine what help he would need long-term and those things.

He wasn't necessarily looking forward to it, but he knew it was one of the necessarily evils of being in the military. He had come out from his last surgery in relatively decent shape, but he also hadn't really figured out what he was supposed to do next.

He was still getting better prosthetics set up, hoping for some that wouldn't make him as sore as what he'd dealt with in the past—and what he was wearing right now for that matter. That's where Kat came in.

The gunman asked, "What the hell are you even doing up here anyway? You managed to get yourself mixed up in shit you shouldn't have."

"Oh, I hear you," Cage replied, looking over at him with a nod. "I came up to find the missing War Dog, and nothing else matters to me."

"But a War Dog matters to you?" he asked, shaking his head. "I guess that's understandable. Damn, those are mighty fine animals."

"Yeah, they sure are," he agreed, "and the little boy who was here, he managed to get one, and he and the dog bonded pretty heavily. He loved that dog."

"Well shit, doesn't that beat all?"

"It happens, and, when the boy had to go to foster care, the dog disappeared."

"Ah, smart dog, and didn't like foster care any more than the next one."

"Probably not. He went to an animal shelter but didn't last there very long at all. He took his leave at the first opportunity."

"Well, I sure as hell hope nobody shot it because that poor animal deserves more than most."

"I agree," Cage replied, "which is what brought me here trying to find him."

"Did you find him?"

"I haven't got my hands on him yet," Cage lied, "but I'm hopeful."

"Yeah, … well, I'm not. The shelter probably put him to death. They do that, you know? When they can't find a place for them within a few days, … they just put them down. It's not as if anybody gets a second chance at life in these places."

"I hope you're wrong," Cage replied, as he continued to move boxes. A dog barked several times in the distance, and it started to irritate the gunman.

"I wish these fucking dogs would just shut the fuck up," he muttered. "That barking just drives into my head."

Cage glanced at him. "Did you ever get that checked?"

"No, I never got that checked. What the hell am I supposed to get checked?" he snapped, glaring at him. "Oh, wait. You're one of those bleeding-heart doctor-believers? Christ, all they do is lie and cheat, trying to make your life something they can make a profit from."

In many ways he wasn't wrong, but it was definitely not always the truth, but no point in arguing with a mentally unstable gunman.

When the dog barked again multiple times, the gunman glared, went to the garage door, and started yelling, "Jesus Christ, that thing needs to shut up. He'll give away that we're here."

Cage shook his head. "He's probably just sounding the alarm that something's off in the neighborhood. It's really not an issue. Just ignore him. Yelling probably makes it worse and calls more attention to you."

"I can't just ignore him. The barking's killing my head." The gunman stared at him. "Why don't you shut him up then, genius?"

"I can try, if you'll let me step over to the door." The gunman nodded, and Cage moved to the door and let out a series of sharp whistles. Almost instantly came silence.

"Well, that worked," the gunman said, looking at him.

"Probably just for the moment because it was different. So no guarantee that it will work long-term," Cage explained. "It's a dog, and he's just doing what they do. It's not human nature but canine nature."

"I just know that he needs to shut the hell up," the gunman muttered. "I don't care what kind of nature he has."

Cage continued to work his way through the boxes, and just as he was opening up another box of what appeared to be clothes, the gunman got pissed. "What is all this shit? It's like stuff from the '80s."

"Well, if your grandfather kept everything, and they weren't exactly the kind to throw out things, it probably wasn't a priority to get rid of."

"Why? Why the hell would anybody want to hang on to this shit?" The gunman moved deeper into the garage, his patience wearing off, and he started flailing around, moving boxes himself.

As Cage made a move toward him, the gun came up and pointed at his face. Cage held up his hands. "I was coming to help."

The gun was lowered, and the gunman pointed. "Move this box over here. It looks to be some personal shit in here." It was personal items but nothing important from many years ago. The gunman swore at it all. "I don't know what the hell I'll do if I can't find it."

Cage didn't say anything and just continued to work, not finding much of anything, and he highly doubted that anybody would keep a diamond or anything else worth a lot of money in a garage and certainly not hidden in this mess. Why the hell would they take a chance of the garage catching on fire or somebody breaking in and taking everything, not knowing what they'd gotten?

Cage's bet was on Oliver selling it, just as he supposedly told the gunman. Just as Fiona talked with her sister about coming into some money. Cage made a mental note to check with Mr. Xavier, the attorney, to directly ask him about any large check recently added to the parents' bank account. Not that Cage would share these thoughts with the gunman.

Instead Cage asked him, "Did you check in and around the bed, under the bed, and all that stuff?"

"Yeah, of course I did," he muttered in frustration. "I went through all the usual spots, but nothing."

Cage just nodded and kept searching through boxes. "Where would you hide it?" he asked the gunman.

"Me? I would have put it in a safe deposit box," he stated.

Cage agreed, adding, "I sure as hell wouldn't keep it in a garage because what if somebody just came and emptied the garage when you weren't here one day or what if a fire burned it all down?"

"Yeah, I've been through the house, and I went through everything. I just had to make it look as if I hadn't been there in case anybody came back."

"Well, you might have looked, but I'm sure there'll be other things that you've missed just because it's the nature of sneaky people who try to hide stuff."

The guy laughed at that. "Everybody tries to hide shit," he agreed. "So maybe it's here among all this crap. I never was very good at hide-and-seek. I'm much more of an upfront kind of guy, as in, *You screw with me, and I'll take you down.*"

"Which you've already proven," Cage noted.

"And that's not our issue for today. Today's issue is the fact that you don't have much time to find this thing."

"Why the hell don't I have much time?" Cage asked, turning to stare at him, his movement fast and certain.

"Because we'll lose daylight, and, if you're out here in the garage with lights on at a place everybody knows is vacant, somebody'll call the cops on you."

"Well, shit," Cage muttered, as he stared around.

The gunman glanced at his watch, just as the dog started barking again. He raised the gun in the direction of the barking, but Cage held up his hands. "Hang on. Let me try to whistle again."

He headed back out and gave another series of sharp whistles. He was pretty sure he'd gotten it right the first time, but the second whistle was a little bit off, so he wasn't sure if Scotty understood. If the dog had that level of training, there was a really good chance that a series of whistles would bring the dog running.

Cage didn't want the War Dog shot by any means, but he needed a distraction, something substantial enough that he could either disappear or could help take out this guy. At the very least, Cage needed a way to get free. The last thing he wanted was to have this guy head to Risa's house.

"You're just trying to get free so you can go back to that chick of yours," the gunman said, waving the gun.

"Wouldn't you go back to your chick?" Cage asked, with feigned surprise. "I mean, how many guys turn down a warm bed for the night?"

"Celine's a little bit on the loose-screw side," he pointed out, "so no. I probably won't head back in that direction anymore."

"I'm sure that will probably break her heart."

"Probably will," he said, with a shrug, "but I don't really give a shit. Plenty of females like her are out there, but not so damn crazy."

"So, you said."

"And I meant it. She was good for information, but, once I told her that there was a murder at the place, she was just fascinated by it. Somehow that always seems to give women a sense of stronger appeal. I never really understood that."

"I don't think all women are like that."

"But this one sure as hell is, and the minute I mentioned the murder, she was all about getting more information, and then she apparently told that girlfriend of yours."

"I don't know that she told her anything. I'm not sure how close of a friendship that is."

"Well, if you listen to the Celine, it's major."

"Well sure, but if you listen to the other, it's not," he pointed out.

The gunman laughed. "Isn't that the truth? But not my problem today. We'll go through this garage until we've found what we're looking for."

Just then came another bark, right inside the garage door.

The gunman jumped and turned, and there was Scotty, wagging his tail all over them. He ran up to Cage and started looking for hugs and love.

He squatted down and gave the dog a big hug. "I presume he escaped his yard," Cage suggested, as he looked over at the gunman.

"He sure as hell doesn't look dangerous, so whatever. Let's get back to work. We're running out of daylight." Not only were they running out of daylight, Cage was running out of time, and his chances of getting out of here anytime soon weren't looking great. He looked down at Scotty and said, "Buddy, you could help us."

"Yeah, right, … as if he'll do that," the gunman snorted.

"Hey, you never know."

Scotty was just happy to be with Cage, as they worked. But Cage didn't want Scotty around this gunman. "I should send the dog home. I don't want him to get into trouble."

"Maybe, but how will you do that? The dog got out. That's all there is to it."

"Maybe, but I should probably send him home." He bent down, gave him a good set of cuddles, and then walked him to the door and ordered him home. Before Scotty left, Cage managed to tuck his card inside the dog's collar, and, with that, the dog took one look and barked at him. When he ordered him off a second time, Scotty took off running.

"Hell, maybe he's smarter than I thought," the gunman said. "At least this way, I don't have to shoot him."

"Shouldn't have to shoot a dog at any time," Cage declared, irritated, as he glanced over at the gunman. "That dog didn't do shit to you."

"Maybe not, but it's not as if he's helping me either."

"Doesn't need to help you. You've had plenty of help right here."

"What the fuck does that mean?" the gunman asked aggressively.

"I'm here. I'm helping."

"Except you haven't found shit though, have you?"

"Maybe not, but I'm working on it."

"Work faster." With that, they continued to move through the boxes, box after box after box.

"Any idea what case it was being kept in or anything?" Cage asked.

"No, nothing. My granddad just talked about it."

At that, Cage frowned at him and asked, "Hang on a minute. Did you ever see it?"

"Of course I fucking saw it. You think I'm a complete loser? I saw it. I don't know where it is, but it's somewhere."

"Good enough," Cage muttered, as he kept working.

Then, all of a sudden, a shout came at the door.

The gunman looked up frantically. "What the fuck?"

And there was the old man, Killian, with Scotty at his side. "Hey, buddy," Killian greeted Cage. "You okay here? I thought I should check out what the fuss was all about."

Cage held up his hand in warning. The old man frowned, not sure what was going on.

Then the gunman came over. "Who the hell are you?" he asked aggressively.

Killian shrugged. "I'm just keeping the dog," he said, looking at the stranger suspiciously. "Who the hell are you? You don't belong here."

"Well, I was the previous owner of this house," he declared.

"Yeah, previous owner doesn't make you an owner," Killian noted pugnaciously, as he shoved his chin forward.

Immediately the gunman pulled out his gun and aimed it at him. "You just shut the fuck up. Otherwise I'll shut you up permanently."

The old man stared at him. "You don't scare me, partner. I've been through too many damn wars to be afraid of that puny little gun."

"Maybe," the gunman conceded, "but I came out of the wars just as damaged as anybody. So, if you want to take me on, you fly right at it. This bullet doesn't care who it takes down."

Cage grabbed Killian's arm and faced the gunman. "Stop. It's fine. He won't hurt anything." The old man just looked at Cage, one eyebrow raised. He gave an ever-so-slight tilt of his head. Cage looked down at the dog. "And look at you, buddy, back again."

"I should just shoot both of them. Too many people are here."

"It's hard to search, that's for sure." Cage looked over at the old man. "Did you ever have anything to do with the family who lived here?"

"No, they weren't the friendliest."

"Yeah, you're not kidding," the gunman snorted.

"But I saw you around here with them quite a bit," Killian noted, looking at him suspiciously.

"You saw me around here every once in a while, not a whole lot."

"Maybe," Killian said, "but you're not exactly the friendly type either, are you? So, what the hell are you doing here now?"

"I left something in the garage, and I'm looking for it," the gunman replied, with a sneer. "Will you do anything about it?"

"No, probably not," he stated, still staring at him, "but it don't look to me as if you're doing anything good either."

"Do you want some old lady's clothes?" he asked, as he held up the contents of the latest box. "We have lots here."

The old man snorted. "I don't, but these people had all kinds of garage sales. I don't think they ever sold much, but they always acted as if everything they had was worth millions."

"Well, some things they had might have been," Cage added, "but, when you look at what's here, most of it is just garbage. Seems these people were trying to make a living out of nothing."

"Yeah, I think so," Killian muttered.

"Did you ever talk to that boy?" the gunman asked Cage.

"No, sure haven't," he said, giving Killian a quick hard look and a tiny, tiny headshake.

"What the hell are you talking about?" the gunman barked. "You were asking all over about that boy."

"I wanted to see the boy and find out if he had anything to say about the missing War Dog," Cage explained. "Haven't tracked him down yet."

"What the fuck would the boy have to do with it?"

"I told you the War Dog was his best friend."

"Yeah, right, as if anybody would just give a War Dog to a kid."

"Obviously not just to a kid, as it required a parent too."

"*Right*," he snorted. "I think it's just all bullshit."

"Maybe, but then again, I'm not so sure the story you've been stringing me along with isn't bullshit too."

At that, the gunman glared at him and barked, "Just keep searching."

Cage shrugged and went back to searching. As he did so, he turned to Killian and suggested, "Just take the dog back home again. It'll probably be for the best."

The old man hesitated, but the gunman added, "Unless you've got a problem with that."

"No, I sure don't," he declared, turning to Cage now. "You sure you'll be okay?"

Cage nodded, and the two exchanged a long gaze, as if both were communicating with the other. Finally Killian just nodded and called the dog, and the two of them slowly walked out.

"Don't know if it's safe to let them go," the gunman growled.

"He's so old, who would ever listen to him anyway?" Cage pointed out. "He's just another damaged vet, an older version of us. Just leave him alone."

The gunman glared at him. "I don't need you fucking

telling me what to do."

"No, apparently you don't," Cage agreed. "Yet you're not doing so well on your own. So let's keep hunting before somebody comes and stops you."

"Nobody'll come and stop me," the gunman snapped. "I'm not going down unless it's in a hail of bullets."

"Do you really need to keep killing people? Is that the only thing on your mind?"

"Yeah, fucking right," he declared. "That's how I feel when people screw me over."

"Well, I'm not against that feeling," Cage noted. "I even understand it to a degree, but it still sucks for anybody who's caught up with you."

"You mean, like you? You think when I'm done here, I'll still go visit that girlfriend of yours?"

"You're just saying shit like that to piss me off," Cage pointed out, raising an eyebrow, "and I can't say I appreciate it."

"As if I fucking care," he spat, glaring at him.

Cage stopped, glared at him, and asked, "So, what do you want to do?"

"What do you mean, *What do I want to do?*"

"You want to fight this out? You want to pop me one, or are we going to look for the damn diamond until you get sick of it or we find it? Then we can go off and do whatever else it is that you want to do."

The gunman stared at Cage for a long moment, then burst into laughter. "Well, damn, most people are scared of guns."

"Most people haven't already been through war the way I have, like the old man. We have a healthy respect for guns, but we're sure as hell not scared of them."

"Right, … got it, my bad." But the gunman was chuckling, as he motioned at the rest of the garage. "You need to keep up the search."

Just then they heard sirens off in the distance.

"What the fuck is that?"

"Who the hell knows?" Cage said, as he bent down and grabbed more boxes. "Jesus, there could be a million reasons for sirens out there."

"If that old man …"

"What? Called the cops to say somebody is picking through a bunch of garbage owned by dead people? Jesus." Cage just glared at him. But when the sirens sounded as if they were coming toward them, it became obvious that the gunman was starting to panic. "Just hang on," Cage muttered, watching the gunman carefully. The last thing Cage needed was to be caught up in a hostage situation.

"If he fucking called the cops, believe me that he'll pay."

"He's so old that anything you do to him will make his life easier."

The gunman frowned at him and groaned. "Well, that takes all the fun out of it."

"Of course it does. Leave the old man alone."

"You care a little too much about that old man."

"I don't care at all. I care about going home to my girlfriend."

"Well, that ain't happening tonight." He raised his gun, pointed it at Cage, and, as he did so, Scotty burst through the door, heading straight for him.

Immediately the gunman changed the direction of the gun, screaming, "Don't you fucking dare!" But the dog was undeterred.

When the first bullet went off, it slammed into the box

that Cage threw as he called off the dog. Almost immediately a huge cacophony came on the other side, and the garage side door burst open. Shots were fired in multiple directions, as Cage grabbed Scotty and pulled him down behind a stack of boxes.

More shooting and screams came from multiple people. Then suddenly came complete silence.

CHAPTER 9

RISA WASN'T SURE what she was supposed to do, but she kept waiting, hoping Cage would show up. That he hadn't contacted her worried the hell out of her. She'd called the police to see if they could do anything, but they had been more than a little flummoxed at the idea of his being taken hostage. Since they didn't know where Cage was, the cops could do absolutely nothing but wait. She had a cop with her still, and, when his phone rang, she jumped up and walked closer.

He just nodded, as he listened to the caller. "Okay, I'll tell her." Then he looked over at her and began, "So …"

"So what?" she snapped. "What happened? What's going on?"

"Cage's been found. I've been told that he's fine and that he's free, but the gunman got away."

She just stared at him. "What do you mean, the gunman got away?"

He shrugged. "I guess there was a bit of a shootout, and, in all the chaos and confusion, he escaped."

"Jesus Christ." She stared at him.

"Yeah, I don't know what to say or what to tell you about it. All I can say is that, at the moment, they're still investigating."

"Right, of course they are." She frowned. "How is that

even possible?"

"Well, the good news is the fact that your partner, your boyfriend, or whatever you want to call him, is free, and he's on his way here. He caught a ride with someone."

"Thank God for that," she muttered, staring at him in shock.

When a knock came on the door not twenty minutes later, she looked over at the policeman still standing guard.

He nodded. "That should be Cage." He walked to the front door, pulled it open, and, sure enough, Cage strode inside.

He took one look at her and walked over and wrapped her up in his arms. "Thank God you're okay," he whispered.

She sighed, as she snuggled in closer. "What the hell is going on?"

"Well, that is a completely different issue, and one we won't get such an easy answer to."

"Are you sure? After all this waiting, I could really use *easy*."

The cop gave them a few minutes and interrupted, "We do have some questions we need to ask."

"Of course." Cage sat down, and, with both of them listening in, he told them what had happened. When he got to the gunman and the dog and the old man, Risa's eyes filled with tears.

"Did he shoot Killian or the dog?" she asked.

"No, he didn't, but not for a lack of trying," Cage noted, with a grim tone.

"Of course," she muttered, "what an asshole."

He chuckled. "I won't say he *wasn't* an asshole, but I will say that he's definitely not on our list of favorites. By the way, Celine has terrible taste in men."

"Ya think?" she muttered. "I can't believe he got away."

"Yeah, I'm not exactly a big fan of that either," Cage noted. "We'll keep an eye out for him because he told me several times that he would be quite happy to come here and to pay you a visit," he shared, with a hard look at the cop.

The cop swore. "We definitely don't want to hear that." He looked over at her. "Do you have somewhere you can go that's safe?"

She looked back at Cage. He nodded and said, "I'll take you to a hotel with me for the night, and we'll go from there."

"Well, you can," the cop said, "but, if you've been followed at all, it won't be a hard thing for our gunman to track you."

"Maybe not, but we can change rooms and go under another name, and we can also change locations," Cage suggested, understanding the cop's suspicions. They were dealing with ex-military, and the gunman was likely good at tracking.

"I just need to know where you'll be at all times," the cop stated. "We can't have you guys disappearing and our not knowing where you are."

"Oh, I agree with you there," Cage admitted, "but I'm more worried about Killian, the old man."

At that, the cop frowned. "I'll talk to the rest of the team about what's being set up for him."

"Well, something definitely needs to be put in place for him," Cage stated. "Killian and that War Dog are the reason I got away."

The cop nodded. "I understand, and obviously we want to confirm that both are as safe as possible."

Risa was not so sure about that, but she was willing to

take it at face value. She wanted to believe that everybody was concerned about Scotty and Killian. By the time the cop left, she looked over at Cage. "Am I really packing an overnight bag?"

He nodded. "You are."

"Where are we going?"

"I'm not sure yet, but how do you feel about going to the old man's house?"

She stared at him. "To look after them or just to confirm they're safe?"

"Kind of both," Cage admitted. "I want to confirm that Killian and Scotty are safe and that, if anybody looks after somebody, that the old man gets looked after."

She frowned at that. "Do you really think they wouldn't?"

"I don't know what to think," Cage noted. "All I can tell you is that I know my gunman will come back again, and I'm afraid he might be pissed off enough to come after the old man and the dog."

She shook her head at that. "And, if we go there, it'll put us all in one spot, and he would have no problem getting at us."

"And," Cage added, with a smirk, "as fate would have it, we'll also set a trap." She winced as he nodded. "It's just a suggestion. I've already been talking to Badger, trying to figure out what our options are."

"Of course you called your boss." She nodded, then shook her head. "Do you think Brian's okay?"

"He should be."

"Do you think he knows anything about the diamond?"

"Well, if he does, he better keep his mouth shut," Cage stated. "I was hoping that it wouldn't come to that, but you're right. With our gunman on the loose, I don't know that Brian is safe either." Cage pulled out his phone and called Badger, filling him in.

Badger asked him, "You're afraid the boy might know?"

"I'm afraid the gunman on the loose might think the boy knows something," he clarified, "and the boy's already vulnerable. So I'm not sure this is something we can ignore."

"No, of course not," Badger agreed. "Let me call my contact in the department, and I'll get back to you."

Cage turned back to her, as she'd been listening in and now stared at him worriedly. "Go pack a bag."

"Right." With a headshake, she hopped up and headed to her bedroom, where she quickly packed an overnight bag. She wasn't sure how long they would be gone, and chances were it would be a little longer than she expected—mostly because it seemed that everything took longer than anybody expected. The fact that this gunman was out there running free even now was very disconcerting.

When she came back out, Cage stood there, his phone in hand again. He smiled at her. "Either we can go say hi to Brian, who has been asking for me, or we can head straight to the old man's house."

"I think we need to do both. I don't want to leave Killian alone after what's happened, or Scotty. Plus, the boy needs protection."

"Seems the police agreed to post an officer with Brian, at least until we have some idea of what's happening with our gunman on the loose. It will make us all feel better when this guy is picked up."

"Sure, but he's also got some crazy-ass skills, doesn't he?"

The smile fell away from Cage's face. "He is military trained. He was discharged as unfit for duty, and, in this case, that means he's having some mental health issues."

"*Great*, so they just discharge him, and he's free to go?"

"There's a certain amount of freedom in that, yes," Cage conceded. "It's definitely one of the loopholes within the military. You can sign out for therapy, and everything goes along tickety-boo, but you don't have to continue with therapy. If there's progress, anybody would sign off on it. So I'm sure he had his ways and means to confirm that it worked out nicely for him."

"It's still a very scary scenario."

"It is, and I won't minimize it," Cage noted, "but we just want everybody out of this and intact. What's really wild is that I'm convinced Oliver already sold the diamond, so no way we can give it to the gunman. He's asking us all to produce this priceless gem that none of us even have."

As they got into her car, she looked back at her apartment, shook her head, and asked, "Do you really think he would come here?"

"Yes, absolutely. Who do you think your Peeping Tom was? I'm also afraid that he might go back to Celine, although he told me that he was done with her."

"What do you mean by *go back to her* then?"

"As in to find out from her who you might be staying with, where you might hang out, things like that. However, … he won't take any of her answers easily. If she's not truthful, he'll hurt her."

"Oh my God," Risa muttered.

"So phone her, give her a partial explanation, and tell her to go stay with some friends, and that friend cannot be you. Not this time."

The phone call was less than fun, and, by the time she was done, Celine was hysterical but heading off to her mother's.

"Good job," Cage said. "Man, she's really a basket case over this."

"She slept with a murderer," Risa pointed out. "So, from her perspective, he could have killed her while she was sleeping."

"Too bad she didn't think about that before she jumped into his bed."

"Honest to God, I don't think she's *ever* thought about it before," she muttered.

"And, while she might be feeling it at this moment, I don't really expect it to change who she is." He gave a chuckle at his own comment, but he knew it was the truth.

"And to a certain extent she's entitled to be who she is and to be happy with it," Risa stated. "It's just such a messed-up world right now that it seems extremely dangerous."

"I won't argue that point," Cage agreed, with a smile in her direction. "Let's just bring this to an end."

"But how? What will you do? Our gunman will be looking for the diamond forever. He's obsessed with …" She stopped and stared at him. "Why don't the cops call him up and let him know they found it? Setting a trap?"

"Yeah, and just let him think the police one-upped him? Everything I'm finding out about our gunman doesn't put him in a good light. There will be hell to pay, and, if I pegged him right, bullets will fly, even at the cops."

"Well, that's no reason to kill him though," she muttered.

"I think it's called self-defense," he joked. "Besides, we can't be nice to people all the time. Yet you're nice to everyone all the time."

"Not really. I haven't been all that nice to you over the years."

"I'm a big boy. I can handle it. I wasn't even thinking I would see you when I came up here this time, but I'm awfully glad I did."

"Good, because I'm not prepared to let you walk away."

"And yet I'll be heading back to my corner of the world when this is done."

"And, just so you know, I'm coming with you." When he gave her a questioning look, she shrugged. "We've been apart for a long time, but, if you're prepared to move forward on the pathway we're already on, I'm not walking away from you."

"Are you sure though? You would have to find a new job and give notice."

"That's fine. I wasn't terribly happy with this one anyway." She rolled her eyes. "Women all over the world need my help."

He chuckled. "I won't argue that one either. I know when I'm beat on that subject."

"Good. It's a relatively new field in physiotherapy, but I won't have any problem getting work, no matter where I go."

"If you say so, and I would absolutely love for you to come with me."

"I think you need to bring Brian too."

Cage totally understood. She was prepared to give him a second chance at life. "We can't save the entire world."

"No, we can't save the entire world," she repeated, "but we do need to save this little boy and Scotty. You know very well that Brian would thrive in your care, and, growing up alongside Jason, Brian would be in heaven."

Cage sighed. "I can't save the entire world."

"No, but what do you think will happen to Brian when his foster parents find out about police protection in their own home?"

He winced at that.

"Exactly," she said. "They'll make Brian's life a living hell, and they'll end up sending him back into the foster care system."

"Maybe," he muttered, "I can't say that would be much fun either way."

Moments later, they pulled up in front of Killian's house. Cage grabbed the overnight bags they had packed and walked up to the front door. When he found the door slightly ajar, his heart skipped a beat. "Shit." He raced inside. She was right on his heels.

When they got to the living room, they found Killian on the ground, unconscious, a head wound bleeding at his temple. Cage dropped to his side and said, "Call 9-1-1."

Risa pulled out her phone, and, looking around, asked, "Where's Scotty?"

"I don't know," Cage replied, "but, if our gunman was pissed at Killian and shot him, then chances are he's also shot the dog."

The old man, outside of the head wound, appeared to be otherwise unscathed and was breathing. Leaving him for Risa to watch over, Cage quickly made a search of the house and headed out to the backyard, where he found Scotty on the ground, also bleeding, with a gunshot wound across the shoulder.

His head was on the ground, but, as soon as Cage approached, his tail wagged. As Cage bent down and checked him over, Scotty lifted his head and whined. "I know, buddy. It's okay. Let's get you up and walking around, so I can see how bad it is."

Getting Scotty up so he could check for injuries, Cage took a good look. The dog moved stiffly, his shoulder obviously hurting, and dried blood was all over his body. When Cage looked back at the house, Risa stood at the back door, her hand over her mouth, an expression of shock and pain on her face. He nodded. "Is there a vet clinic in the area?"

"I'll look," she said, pulling out her phone. She quickly located one and came to his side. "Found one. We need to get him right over there. You go."

He shook his head. "Not until the paramedics are here for Killian."

"They're already here," she replied. "They're just getting to the front door now."

They raced to the front door and let them in, and chaos followed for the next twenty minutes, while they got Killian ready for transport. Once the ambulance pulled away, they got back into Risa's vehicle, with the dog in the back seat. They went to the vet and were seen right away.

As soon as they got into the waiting room, they were immediately moved into an exam room, where Cage explained what had happened.

Scotty was gently put on the exam table, where the doctor took a quick look. He nodded and shared, "Well, I'm not sure whether this dog was really good at playing dead or what, but this was definitely a lucky shot."

"I'm not sure how much of it was a lucky shot as much as the guy didn't really want to kill the dog," Cage muttered. "Maybe if the dog understood, he *was* playing dead," he suggested, with half a smile.

"I'm glad to hear it either way, because Scotty will be just fine." The doctor checked him all over again for any other injuries. "He will be sore though, and may need some pain meds for the next few days. You'll want to keep him moving, or that shoulder will stiffen up quickly."

"Got it," Cage noted.

When the exam was over, they moved Scotty back out to the car. As they got in, Risa asked, "Now where?"

He hesitated, looking over at her. "How do you feel about taking Scotty over to see Brian for a meeting?"

"You know it'll be hard on the boy when they're separated again."

"I know," he agreed. "I just think it will be a good thing for both of them. I know it will give the dog a healing boost, and no doubt Brian too."

She hesitated, then nodded. "I think you're probably right on that score, but it might be much harder afterward."

Deciding that would be the best answer, they drove to the foster home, where Brian was staying. As they got up to the front of the house, the front door burst open, and there was Brian in his wheelchair, staring at Scotty, tears streaming down his face.

The two had an emotional reunion in the entryway to the house. At times it was uncomfortable for Scotty, as they had to remind Brian repeatedly about the dog's injury. It was quite the sight as the boy couldn't stop crying. Meanwhile, the police were there, standing guard over him. Dorothy stood horrified in the corner, and the father seemed to be completely out of his depth.

Cage knew instinctively that this would be the last straw and that Brian would be going back to foster care. He pulled out his phone and contacted his brother. They talked for a minute, but Jason was called away. However, that conversation needed to continue and soon.

When his brother called back a little bit later, Jason spoke with a smile in his tone. "I'm not at all surprised."

"I am," Cage quipped, "because this is foolishness."

"No, it's part of who you are, bro, so don't knock it. You've always been a great one for this, so own it. I do have a contact who might make things a little easier, and, if you can get Badger to pitch in, I think you'll find it much easier to process this quickly."

"I don't know," Cage grumbled. "There'll be a trial period, and you know, if for some reason it doesn't work out, that'll devastate everybody." Cage was scared, which was an uncommon feeling, and this was a completely different danger than he was used to dealing with. "So, no trial. … Sink or swim, we deal with it. This is what we know and understand."

With that agreed to, Jason disconnected.

Putting wheels in motion that in no way that Cage understood, he was dreading it all on the inside and had no idea how it all would work out or what the process would be.

At that point, the foster father stepped forward, looking completely shook up. "This is an untenable situation here," he told to the officer. "We didn't sign up for any of this."

"Of course not," the officer noted, trying to get him to calm down. "Obviously nobody expected this to happen."

"Well, if we'd realized that his family was murdered, I don't think we would have gone in this direction." Jameson looked over at Dorothy, his wife, who shook her head.

It was obvious to everyone that they just wanted them all gone.

Cage turned to Brian, who still had his arms wrapped

around Scotty, crying quietly but with occasional body-heaving sobs. Cage bent down and wrapped his arms around the little boy. "Hey, Brian, no need to worry, bud. We found Scotty, and he's hurt, but he'll be just fine."

He nodded. "And he went home. He's always been really good at that."

"Going home?"

"Yeah, going home," Brian said, with tears in his voice, "but I don't know what'll happen to him now."

"I'm not sure either," Cage replied. "I'll probably keep him with me for the time being, while I sort out what happens next."

The little boy looked up at him expectantly. "Does that mean you can bring him to visit?"

At that, Jameson came forward, "There will be no visiting here. I'm afraid this is the end for us. We weren't sure that we could do this in the first place, but this is a definite no." Dorothy stood behind him, nodding, glanced around at everybody. "This is just too much. Arrangements need to be made for Brian to go back to the center."

Brian cried out in such pain that Cage grasped his shoulders in support. He looked over at the foster parents. "This hardly changes anything."

"Of course it does," Jameson argued, red in the face. "It changes everything for us. There's now a madman after him, and all he'll want to do is pine away for that dog," he added, looking at Scotty in disgust. "And I can assure you that won't happen here. I don't want that dog in the house."

"This dog is very well trained," Cage explained, trying, but knowing it was futile. "It's a War Dog and one of the best guardian dogs you could ever have."

"Well, it didn't do him any good now, did it?" he

snapped.

"This dog has been a huge help to me, as he saved my life earlier today."

"Then you take it," Dorothy snapped. "We don't want it here."

"I'm sorry you feel that way."

She sniffed, her head going up into the air. "That means nothing. This is ridiculous. We were looking for a way to make some money, not deal with all this. It's way more than anybody could be expected to handle."

"I don't think Brian expected to handle a lot of things that have come his way either," Cage pointed out.

She just stared at him with an unforgiving look in her eyes, and he realized that, as far as she was concerned, this really was it. Brian was heading back to a center, regardless of what anybody thought.

When a hand slipped into his, he realized it was Brian's. He looked down at him and smiled. "Well, you know what they say. When one door closes, another door opens."

"Maybe for other people," Brian whispered. Tears filled his eyes as he kept one hand wrapped tightly on the ruff of the dog, who even now looked as if he'd found his home again, leaning up against Brian's wheelchair. "All we ever wanted was to be home."

"I understand," Cage told the little boy, "but I'm afraid that home as you knew it is gone."

Tears slipped down Brian's face as he nodded. "I know," he whispered, "but it's not fair."

"No, it's not fair, life is never fair in a deal like this." Cage wasn't sure what to do right now.

The officer walked over to them and announced, "I'll have to call social services."

Cage just nodded, not knowing what else to do. Even if he wanted to try, right now there was still the problem of the gunman. "Is anybody keeping an eye on the perimeter of the house?" he asked in a low tone.

"I would imagine so, but I'm not privy to the plan as to what's going on," the cop replied, "but I believe that was taken into consideration."

Then a voice at the doorway interrupted, "How about I just kill him, and then we won't have to worry about it at all?"

Cage turned ever-so-slowly to see Adam Harland, the gunman, standing there at the doorway, staring at them with a grin on his face.

The officer went for his handgun, but Adam fired a shot, dropping him so quickly that nobody really realized what had happened.

Immediately Dorothy screamed at the top of her lungs, and, after disarming the injured officer, Adam turned his attention to her.

"Wait," Cage yelled out.

Adam turned and looked at him. "You shut her up then. Otherwise I will."

Wincing, Cage walked over to the woman, who was now screaming uncontrollably, her husband trying ineffectually to calm her down. Cage reached back with one hand and slapped her hard across the face.

She collapsed to the ground, sobbing quietly, huddled in a pile on the floor. Her husband crouched beside her, glaring at him. "You didn't have to hit her so hard."

"I couldn't just let this guy shoot her either."

"You should have let me shoot her," Adam stated ruefully. "What the hell are you doing here anyway?" Then he looked at Scotty and glared. Scotty immediately growled, his hackles up. "If that thing attacks me, I'll shoot to kill. I took it easy on the dog last time, thinking maybe he would take it as a warning, but I won't let it deter me this time. So that's all the warning it's getting."

"I hear you," Cage replied. "No need to start shooting."

"Oh, look. There's your pretty little girlfriend," Adam said giddily. "I'm so happy we're all having a lovely reunion."

At that, the little boy in the wheelchair sat up straight and whispered, "Did you kill my parents?"

He looked at him and sighed. "Yeah, I did. Sorry about that, dude. Life isn't exactly a bed of roses, and your parents were not very nice people. They stole something from me."

"That's not true," Cage stated. "Brian doesn't need his good memories of his parents smeared, just so you can twist it all around to suit your narrative."

"As if I give a shit," Adam snapped, with an eye roll. "But now we have a problem." He walked over to the little boy, leaned down in front of him. "Your parents had something of mine that I want back. So you give it back to me, and everything will be fine."

Brian just stared up at him in shock. "I don't know anything about that. What did they have?"

"Well, I'm really hoping that's not true. You see, ... I really need it back, and we've gone through all that crap in the garage, and there's still no sign of it. So, I'm asking nicely. ... What is it that you know that I don't? It might just save your life."

Brian stared up at him, his eyes huge, Scotty was at his side, still growling. Adam just waved his gun at him. "Shut him up."

Immediately the little boy grabbed the dog and held him

close to still him, Cage commanded Scotty to keep still. Scotty subsided.

"It's too damn bad," Adam said, "that we have to hurt such a damn good dog like him again."

"You don't have to hurt him again. He's a dog," Brian wailed. "He's my dog. I don't want anything to hurt him."

"Then tell me where your parents kept the diamond."

Brian looked at him and frowned. "I don't know what a diamond is."

With that, Adam just sighed and closed his eyes, then turned to look at Cage. "I don't want to hurt him, but I need that diamond."

"I know you do," Cage noted, "but, honest to God, nobody knows where it is. Did you ever consider that maybe they were lying?"

He stared at Cage, the color fading from his face. "They better not have been. You've got to understand, … I need it."

"You might need it," Cage conceded, "but there's no guarantee it will even be possible to find. For all I know, Oliver being the kind of guy he was, … he may have beat you to it, if he ever had it at all."

"He would too," Adam agreed, staring off in the distance. "Oliver was just that kind of an asshole." He slowly walked toward the door, then turned back and announced, "I can't let you guys live."

"And we can't let you shoot everybody," Cage murmured.

Adam stepped through the door, looked back, then raised his gun. Just then a series of shots were fired. Cage yelled for everyone to duck and threw himself in front of Brian as he watched Adam's body dance in midair, then fall to the ground, as cops outside took advantage of the opportunity and took him down.

Cage looked around to see everyone frozen in place, but nobody else had been hit. He turned and raced to Adam's body, kicked the gun out of reach, and bent down to check him.

He lifted a hand to the police standing outside and shouted, "The gunman's dead, and we have a downed officer. Otherwise nobody else in here has a weapon."

Immediately the place was swamped with armed officers. After a quick search, things calmed down, and the little boy was shaking beside Cage. Risa had her arms wrapped around Brian, holding him close, telling him it would be okay.

She looked up at Cage with tears in her eyes. Then he bent down and wrapped both of them in his arms.

Brian burrowed against Cage's chest, sobbing, and Scotty even pushed his nose up in between them to confirm that he was getting his cuddles too. When the sobs finally slowed down, Cage looked over at the officers waiting for him.

"We have a bunch of questions that need to be answered," Detective Hendricks stated.

Risa groaned. "Honest to God, I just want to go home."

"Home?" Cage asked.

She looked at him and shook her head. "No, you're right. I'm done. It's time to go to your home."

"Ha, not sure about that, but we'll see."

The questions and answers took a fair bit, and, by the time child services showed up, they were all curled up on the couch.

Brian was out of his wheelchair and curled up in Cage's arms, and his lap was pretty full. With Scotty at their feet, the entire clan had glommed on to him, and he couldn't be happier, but he also knew that there wouldn't be an easy way to make this happen. There would be a hell of a lot of paperwork and bureaucracy to go through, and he also didn't know if there was a better answer for Brian.

He wasn't parent material necessarily, and it wouldn't be an easy thing to convince anybody to place the boy with a single parent with the challenges and work history Cage had. Another knock on the door had the police going to answer it, instead of the homeowners, who looked as if they were completely at their wit's end.

Cage looked over at the new arrival and groaned. "Seriously?"

"Yeah, seriously," Jason declared, as he rolled in.

Immediately Brian perked up and looked over at him with interest. "Wow, that's a cool-looking wheelchair."

"It is, isn't it?" Jason said, rubbing his hands together. "I'm Jason, Cage's brother," he told Brian. "Cage wasn't kidding if he told you that I was in a wheelchair, and I've been here a long time."

"Wow," Brian muttered, as he leaned in to look closer at the racing stripes that Cage himself had painted on the wheelchair. "Holy cow," he said, still stunned. "Do you think I could have one like that?"

"Well, not quite yet, but, when you're bigger, why not?" Jason replied, as he looked over at the couple who were talking furiously with the social services representative. "I gather quite a headache is going on here."

Brian shrugged and hung his head. "They don't want me. I don't think they ever did."

"Well, that's a good thing," Jason announced, with a big bright smile, and that turned all heads his way.

"How is that a good thing?" Brian asked, almost in tears.

"I really don't want to go back into the institute or that center. There were lots of people like me, but it feels better to be part of a family, even if it's not perfect."

A sob came from behind him, and Cage looked over to see tears running down Risa's face. He reached out a hand and squeezed hers gently. "God, it just breaks my heart," Risa whispered. "The damage that asshole did." Realizing what she had said in front of Brian, she added, "Oops, sorry about that."

Brian looked at her and shrugged. "He was an asshole."

She gave him a bright smile. "Hey, language, please, and maybe that's true," she acknowledged, "but that will be the one and only time we allow swearing. You've got to watch that mouth of yours."

He looked at her steadily. "Yeah, what will you do about it?"

She chuckled. "Young man, you have no idea how your life is about to change." She glanced over at Jason. "I presume you're behind this?"

"Me? Come on. No, how could I possibly be behind anything?" he teased, with a big laugh in her direction. "Anyhow, it's nice to see you and my brother together."

"I swear to God, we were just idiots," she muttered.

"You sure were," Jason agreed, staring her down steadily. She glared at him, and he just shrugged, completely unrepentant. "Think about it," he began. "All the times that you wondered and worried, but instead of picking up the damn phone and calling him, you just sat back and watched it all go away."

"He could have contacted me too, though, as far as he knew, it was a done deal. On the other hand, he didn't have to listen to my mother."

"Maybe not," Jason admitted, "so we give both of you demerits for being idiots."

"*Gee thanks*," Cage replied in a dry tone.

Just then the child services social worker walked over, wearing the biggest frown she could have possibly worn. Cage looked at her and quickly extricated himself from the people and dog in his arms and stood up.

Staring at him and watching the scene carefully, she stated, "I think we need to talk."

"Sounds good," he said comfortably, and he walked a short distance away.

The social worker eyed Brian, who was now getting settled back in his wheelchair. "I was really hoping things would work out here, but I don't think this foster family was quite ready for this."

"No," Risa agreed.

The social worker nodded. "I did wonder at the time, but they were pretty eager."

Risa added, "I think they were more concerned about the paycheck and not so much for the child."

She nodded. "We have a lot of people go into this because they think they'll make enough money to help themselves out but don't realize just how much work is involved. As it is, that boy appears to be pretty happy with your family over there."

Cage nodded. "No reason for him not to be, and he will be welcomed as one of us."

"And yet," the social worker stated in a firm voice, "you don't just get to keep him."

His back stiffened, as he waited for the inevitable onslaught of bureaucracy that he had been dreading.

"There are processes, background checks, paperwork, all

kinds of things, and you will need references."

Eyeing her playfully, he asked, "Are you telling me that you haven't got a million references already?"

She rolled her eyes at that. "I'm not sure anybody has ever come in with quite so many references, but it's not a done deal. You're also talking about going to a district that isn't mine."

"True, but, if you allow it, you know perfectly well that they will take it up on the other side."

She frowned. "Sure, but I'm not sure I'm comfortable with this."

"And what is it you're uncomfortable with?"

She studied the scene, only just realizing that someone else was in a wheelchair. "Who is that in the wheelchair?"

"My brother," Cage replied. "He's been in it since he was eight." She frowned at that, and he nodded. "If anybody in this room has the experience to deal with whatever Brian's going through, it's the two of us."

"Maybe," she muttered, "but that's not necessarily enough."

"It might not be enough to you, but I can tell you that it's a really good start." She was still frowning when he leaned over and added, "You might as well just give in because none of us are prepared to let that boy stay here, where he's not wanted, or to go back to an institution."

"But you've never raised a child."

"You don't understand my story, so let me tell you. … That is my brother Jason, and we lost our parents, by the way. He is a high-level basketball player, and he'll be legit very soon. Sure, he is handicapped, but he will be in the Paralympics or Para-whatever they decide to call it this year," Cage declared, waving his hands, "because Jason is that good.

And, just like Jason, Brian will be welcomed just as he is, for who he is, and, if anybody can keep him safe, it will be me and Jason and that War Dog."

"And the dog," she repeated, her eyes widening as she recognized Scotty. "Is that his dog?"

"It is." Cage smiled broadly. "And I've got to tell you, that dog is exactly what that boy needs right now."

"Oh, so now you'll tell me you have room for the dog too?" she asked, with a disbelieving tone.

He frowned at her and said, "I get the feeling that, in your work, you don't have too many happy endings."

"No," she agreed. "More often than not, people are out for themselves. They start with good intentions, but it doesn't last, and the children suffer."

Cage nodded. "Well, if that were the case with me, I would have ditched my brother a long time ago." He turned and looked back at Jason. "Hey, Jase. I should have dumped you a long time ago, right?"

Jason turned and snorted. "You should have, but too late now, bro. We're family, and that's all that matters. Besides, I would kick your ass if you ever did."

She groaned. "And why the hell do I have recommendations here from people incredibly high up in the military?" She eyed Cage carefully, expecting an appropriate answer. "Who the hell are you?"

"Somebody who is more than ready to take on that little boy," he replied, "and the War Dog is coming with us too."

"What do you mean, coming with you?" she asked in alarm.

Cage announced, "I'm taking the whole lot of them back home." She was still sputtering when he added calmly, "You need to make the paperwork happen and fast, so we can get out of here. That boy needs a chance to go out and play with his dog, and remember that we're doing this *for him.*"

"Yes, but you're a single man, and that's not good enough."

He frowned. "What do you mean, it's not good enough?"

She let out a slow breath, trying hard for control. "There are checks and balances, and, in a case like this, we can't just hand him off to somebody just because you think it's a good idea. He's not a pet."

He glared at her. "I'm not sure anybody in this room is more aware of that than I am, and I'm also fully aware that, although there are challenges to being a single parent and looking after somebody like Brian, it is not impossible."

"No, of course it's not impossible, but it is a challenge, and it's a challenge that you are just starting."

He gave her a dry look and stated, "You probably should check your emails again."

She frowned and pulled out her phone, her eyes widening as she saw the emails rolling in still. She rubbed at her furrowed brow. "I've never seen anything like this."

"I'm a decorated military veteran. I have a lot of great references. I'm highly experienced in a variety of situations, and I really don't think the fact that I don't have a wife makes a damn bit of difference."

"Well, how about a wife in training?" Risa asked, as she slipped her hand into his.

He looked down at her, smiled, then pulled her up close and kissed her.

The child services woman watched the two of them suspiciously.

Cage explained, "We were together a long time ago, and

my military service pulled us apart. We've just reconnected."

"Yes, but you're not engaged, and you're not ready to get married," she noted, "so that's a whole different story."

"It's not even part of the story," Cage argued, "because it has nothing to do with love. If you were able to let this wonderful kid go to somebody with zero experience and no empathy, just because at one time their house was wheelchair accessible, I'm not sure what other criteria you possibly had for this placement of Brian with Jameson and Dorothy. If you did that, then you can certainly give him a chance with us, who already love him. He was on a trial period here. Brian can come permanently to my place, him and Scotty."

At that came a shocked gasp, and Cage turned to see Brian staring up at him, with hope in his eyes. "Do you mean it?"

He nodded. "Of course I mean it. Besides, we will have a hell of a time talking my brother out of taking you home right now. He figures he'll have another basketball player on his court."

"I love basketball," Brian said. "I just can't play anymore."

Jason shook his head. "That's all right, dude. We play all the time."

"You *play*, play?"

"Sure, obviously we have wheels, and it's not exactly the same thing, but yeah, we *play*, play. We'll get you out on the court in no time. Cage put a court in for me at home."

At that, Brian turned to look at Cage, his eyes wide. He looked from the social worker, over to Cage, then back again. "Please," Brian said, with a hint of desperation. "I'm so uncomfortable everywhere else. Nobody understands me. Nobody understands what I'm going through, and no one else wants me," he whispered. "It's just so hard."

The social worker frowned, trying to stay businesslike in the face of those pleas. Then she groaned. "Look …"

"No," Cage interrupted, "it's really simple. We have a home, a safe and loving home, and Brian and Scotty are welcome to come be a part of the family. We'll show Brian how to make that wheelchair become something that's a part of him, that he can learn to thrive in. And, if any surgery is down the road, we will do anything to make his life easier. We'll get it done, and we'll all be there for him."

She stared at him. "You talk a good talk, but …"

"No buts," he declared, with a bright smile. "Feel free to come by in a year, or any time that you want to visit."

She frowned. "I would have to because I couldn't live with myself."

And that's when he realized that her whole reason for struggling so much was because she didn't know Cage, didn't know what his home life was like, and didn't know if this was the right thing to do or not.

"I'm not sure what it would take to convince you that this is the right thing, and I understand that it needs to be a decision you're totally comfortable with," Cage began. "So follow us home. It won't be tonight though, as Killian, an older neighbor of Brian's, is in the hospital. However, once we are assured that Killian is okay, we plan to leave sometime this week. It's about two hours away, if we get stuck in traffic. You'll know in just a few days how you feel about our situation. Then set another time to visit, giving Brian time to learn to shine and to love who he is in this life. You can check in on us as often as you like. If ever you think he's not doing well enough to meet your expectations, we'll find a way to change and to improve it. I guess in that case you would have some tangible reason for what you're worrying about right now."

She stared at him, miserable and confused.

He looked over at the two boys in wheelchairs, one big and one little. Now Brian was in Jason's arms, giggling as his brother picked him up and tossed him gently. It was obvious that Brian was very underweight and needed some muscle building and nutrients, but, more than that, he needed to know he was loved. He needed to know he was secure and that somebody had his back. Cage pointed the social worker to the two boys.

The woman was struggling so hard to commit to a decision here.

"We're the good guys here," Cage declared. "We want Brian and Scotty with us. We just want to give him and his dog a home, a loving home." She pinched her lips, then he nodded. "You could just tell your boss that I've kidnapped him, and that's how it went down."

She rolled her eyes at that. "That won't do any good."

"You never know," he said cheerfully. Cage looked over at Brian. "You would be okay to come home with us, wouldn't you?"

Brian nodded eagerly. "Oh yes, … please. … Can I? I just want to go home with them." He wrapped his arms around Jason's neck and hung on tight.

Jason chuckled with laughter and added, "I'm taking him outside. This kid needs to get out of this atmosphere. It's stifling." And, with that, he headed over to the front steps.

"Wait, no ramps are there," the social worker cried out. "He can't get down there."

"You don't know Jason," Cage countered. "Come and

watch, as this is how we operate in *my* world."

She quickly moved to the front door just in time to see Jason carefully navigating the wheelchair down the stairs, perfectly fine, with Brian holding on tight.

When they hit the bottom, the two of them turned to look back up at the rest of them at the front door and waved.

"Good God," she muttered, "he really does know how to make that thing work, doesn't he?"

"Not only how to make it work but how to make it his, and that's the big difference. My brother may not get out of that wheelchair, but we still have hope. I don't know about Brian's medical condition, and that's something that I would need to look at with specialists, in case there is anything we can do for him," Cage explained. "However, I can tell you that we're willing and happy to do whatever it takes."

CHAPTER 10

THE NEXT MORNING, Cage and Risa and Jason and Brian stopped in to see Killian at the hospital. Scotty had a follow-up visit with the vet and was at the clinic, waiting for them to pick him up. Thankfully Killian was now conscious and cheerful. He was delighted to see the whole lot of them.

"You know, I would move closer to be with you too if I thought I could find a place," he offered, shaking his head. "Being alone at this age sucks."

Immediately Cage laughed. "Tell you what, … we've got a trailer on the property. It's not new by any means and could use a little cleaning up, but you're more than welcome to come join us."

The old man stared at him in astonishment. "Seriously?"

"Sure, why not? It's not as if we have anything else to do with the place. You're right. It sucks to be alone when you're old, but it also sucks to be alone when you're young," Cage said gently, "and this little guy could use a grandpa."

At that, Jason and Brian wheeled over, and Brian lifted up his arms. Killian leaned over and gave him a hug. Tears were in Killian's eyes as he muttered, "I don't know how I would make that happen."

"We have a place for you. That's all you need to know. Sell your house and get whatever you can for it, so you've got something to live off of, along with your pension. Then come on down our way," Cage suggested. "And, if you need a hand, we'll make that happen too."

By the time they left, Brian was over the moon with joy, and Jason was laughing. "Look at that, a ready-made family, including a grandpa."

"Don't knock it," Cage reminded him. "That old man saved our lives."

"Oh, I'm not knocking it," Jason noted. "I'm just thrilled for you. Dude, now I can leave you guys alone when I'm off on my trips, knowing you'll be okay."

Brian turned to him and asked, "You're not leaving, are you?"

"No, not leave as in *leave forever*," he explained, "but I'm on a professional basketball team now, so some days I have to go away for training camps and road games."

"Wow." Brian was totally in awe.

At that, there would be no end to Brian's adulation for Jason, or Cage's for his brother. Jason understood because he had survived so much himself, and he couldn't be happier.

RISA PICKED UP Cage's hand resting on the gear shift, and she squeezed his fingers and as they drove along. "That was a hell of a leap," she stated, smiling broadly. "At least your vehicle is getting fixed, finally, and I love they are going to leave it parked at 'grandpa's' place until we get back for it."

"It was, wasn't it?" he said quite comfortably. "This way we can keep an eye on his progress over the next week or two as well."

"I don't think your boss was expecting all this."

Cage thought about it and laughed. "No, I'm pretty sure my boss did not expect *all* of this, but you've got to understand her, … him, … them," he began. "Badger and Kat? They roll with all these punches, and, if this is what I want to do, they'll be there for us."

"Wow, you're showing me a side of life I've never seen, and a certain kind of people I've never met before."

"Yeah, and just think. You're the one who walked away from it years ago."

"Oh, I don't know about that," she countered. "I didn't really walk as much as I didn't understand what was going on." Just then she got a call from Graham. "Oh my gosh," she greeted him. "I totally forgot, but I'll have to break our dinner date for next week."

"Why?" Graham asked in disappointment. By the time she got through explaining everything, he was over the moon in happiness for her. "Don't worry. I get down that way all the time, so maybe we could make it another day, if you are still up for it?"

Picking up a note of hesitation in his voice, she smiled as she replied, wanting to reassure him. "Absolutely. I definitely want to spend more time together and do a much better job of keeping in touch. Plus, I've got some people I want you to meet. Sorry, my news took over the call. Was there a specific reason you phoned me?"

"Yes," he replied, with a chuckle. "I wanted to tell you that, after much discussion with Eleanor, via her lawyers of course, she has agreed that the money I had given her for your education and the down payment for a house is all being transferred to you as intended. The lawyers are handling it, so I'm confident you should see that show up in your bank account pretty quickly."

"What?" Risa was ecstatic, yet in shock. Her mother was not one for compromises, and definitely not prone to doing the right thing where money was concerned.

Graham explained, "At the end of the day I don't think your mother wanted to trust her luck in court. Not when we had contracts in place for these kinds of things," he shared. "I had no idea that she would be the type of person to keep it from you, and I'm very sorry you had to deal with that. But now, with the chance that it could all come out in court and potentially damage her credibility in the midst of settling our other business, she is backing down."

"Wow," Risa muttered, stunned, as she stared over at Cage.

"So, as long as you're okay with it, I would really like to stay in touch. It would be something for me to look forward to."

"Oh my goodness, of course. I'm sorry we lost touch in the first place. Mother always pointed out that I needed her because nobody else wanted anything to do with me. That was one of the hardest things for me, and I was just foolish enough to believe her."

"Now you know better," Graham stated. "I'll give you a week or two to get settled, and then I'll hop on down, and we'll go out for lunch."

When he ended the call, she stared at her phone, feeling the tears in the back of her eyes. Taking a deep breath, she got her emotions under control and told Cage all about it.

"That's really great. Any idea how much it was?"

"No, I have no idea, but the amount doesn't even matter. It's the whole idea of it. I'm just shocked."

"The reality is, Graham had Eleanor over a barrel. So you should probably give your mother a wide berth for a while."

"I planned to give her a wide berth for a long time anyway," Risa replied. "Finding out what she did was hard enough. Then remembering how I struggled financially while going through school, yet she did nothing, really stings. She even went out of her way to misrepresent her own situation, which makes me want to have nothing to do with her. I definitely need to give it some time," she muttered. "I'm just now realizing how much Celine was like my mother."

He nodded. "Yep, you don't need toxic people who lie to you in your life. Now keeping in touch with Graham, that sounds good, and it seems your stepdad really wants to stay in touch."

"Yes, he said as much, and I believe him," she said. "I really liked him, and it broke my heart when they split up. And, of course, a break up between parents is really tough on the kids, no matter their age, even in the best of cases, and this situation was anything but. It's a tough world to be a kid out there."

"It is," Brian agreed from the back seat. "It really is."

All the adults laughed at that, and Risa smiled at Cage. "It's a pretty decent day all around."

"Good, keep that in mind when we finally get to the chaos at home."

It wasn't a terribly long drive, and a couple of hours later they pulled up to the same old farmhouse she remembered. She sighed happily. "I forgot how beautiful it is here."

Brian poked his head through the side window and asked, "This place is yours?"

"Yeah, and now it's yours too. This was the home where Jason and I grew up. Our parents left it to us."

"Oh, wow, this is cool."

That was just another thing for Cage to remember, as he needed to check with the lawyers to confirm this boy got his inheritance too, but that was an issue for tomorrow.

Right now, it was a case of getting everybody settled.

HOURS LATER, AFTER Brian and Jason had played on the basketball court until the sun went down, everybody then ate dinner and afterward disappeared to bed for the night. Scotty was incredibly protective, but seemed to absolutely love being with everybody here.

Despite his injury, Scotty found the basketball court fun and the basketball itself very confusing, trying to steal it from them constantly, but it was too big for his jaw. At the end of the day, they had to pull him out of the game and give him some balls of his own—tennis balls—which he thought were pretty perfect. Now the dog was following them all around, making sure that everybody was exactly where they needed to be.

Cage smiled as he patted Scotty. "It's okay, boy. This is home for you now too."

Scotty gazed up at him, almost a look of acknowledgment, a look suggesting that he had this now. Then he settled in a huge dog bed in the middle of the hallway, where he could watch everybody come and go. With the deepest heaviest sigh, he relaxed, probably for the first time in a very long time.

Risa came up beside Cage, wrapped her arms around him, and whispered, "That's an awful lot of good done today."

"It was, wasn't it?" he said. "What do you think about Killian?"

"I think he seemed really happy to join us soon, but we can't let it go too long, or he'll get to feeling as if he's not welcome. I want to bring some of my furniture down here, and I thought maybe he and I could share a moving truck and help him make it happen."

"Depends on how much stuff you've got," Cage noted, "but we can work out those details." He pointed through the living room window to a decent trailer with a big deck off it across the yard. "That's the trailer I'm talking about."

She smiled and nodded. "That's perfect, and Brian will love having Killian close by. Scotty too."

"Yep, and I think all three of them will be pretty happy here." He looked down at her and kissed her gently. "What about you? Are you okay with all this?"

"I am okay. It's a lot of change. It's a lot of new and different. It feels as if everything's been tossed up and dropped into a completely chaotic mess," she shared, "but that's okay too. It feels pretty darn fine. But one thing we have to settle up."

"What's that?" he asked.

"Where am I sleeping?"

"Ah, I do have a bedroom upstairs for you."

"Oh, that's nice." She wrinkled up her nose. "I hope that it's yours." He looked down at her and frowned. She ran her fingers across his lips and asked, "Now what's the frown for?"

"I didn't want to push it too fast."

"Push away," she said, laughing. "Since I found you again, I haven't let go one bit. So, if anybody's pushing, it's me. Honest to God, I'm not even really pushing. I'm just letting you know that I'm not letting go." He hesitated and she nodded. "I know you think it's too much, too fast, too something"—she rolled her eyes—"and you always were a bit of a worry wart. You were always asking me if I was okay with the speed of things. Apparently you've forgotten that I was the one who usually pushed you a little faster each time."

He chuckled as he pulled her into his arms and held her close. "I haven't forgotten. I was trying to put all that out of my mind and give you time."

"Silly you," she muttered, with a headshake.

"Not silly," he argued. "I was thinking of you."

"Yeah, I know you were," she said, with a smile. "Always considerate, always there for us, but, in this instance, I have no intention of being a fool any longer. I don't know what I was thinking when I allowed my mother to trick me into believing everything she said, but there it is. Only as I left home and finally sorted out who I am on my own did anything start to make sense."

"I'm glad it's all making sense," he replied, with a smile, "because that's important."

"It is," she murmured. "One of the things that I'm very clear on is the fact that I was a fool to not follow up. I was a fool to have believed her and just to assume I wasn't wanted. ... I was a fool to let you go—and Graham, for that matter, but I am not too proud to admit it. I did finally figure it out, and, honest to God, I couldn't be happier." He looked at her for a long moment, and she nodded. "And, before you ask, I am sure."

He smiled, leaned down, and kissed her intently, until she sagged against him. "In that case, I really do think we need to go upstairs."

"Oh, I agree," she teased and pecked him playfully.

When they got up to his room, she walked in and

stopped, then started to laugh. "You already put my things in here?"

"Well, I was kind of pushing it and wasn't sure I should be rushing you, but it's where I thought you belonged. We've already had enough time apart."

"No kidding," she replied, with a smile. "We've had way-too-much time apart." She wrapped her arms around him and added, "And this is just perfect."

"Good," he murmured, "I was hoping it would be." He picked her up, carried her over to the bed, and whispered, "You're right. We've lost *way*-too-much time."

He went to give her another kiss, but she shook her head. "I need a shower."

"Oh, right."

She stepped back, walked to the bathroom, then turned to look at him. "Of course you could always join me." He looked down at his leg, and she nodded. "You need to get out of that thing, don't you?"

"I do, so you go have a shower, and I'll join you. How's that?" He watched as she walked away, realizing this would be the first time she'd seen his prosthetic and his stump. It wasn't so much that he was bothered, yet he didn't want her to be bothered, and that was a whole different thing.

As he sat down on the side of the bed, he thought about it and realized that a chair was not very far away. If he put it outside the bathroom, that would make it a whole lot easier for him.

He quickly moved the chair, then sat down and stripped off his clothes as much as he could, slowly took off the prosthetic, groaning with relief as his muscles had a chance to relax and to shift.

He absolutely loved the freedom the prosthetic gave

him, but also something was so limiting about it that he loved taking it off too. With that off, he quickly rolled down the sock, wincing at the redness and swelling underneath. He really needed to go back on crutches for a day or two, but he was also pretty damn stubborn about that. He stood, grabbed the one crutch he had placed to the side, and, using that, he made his way to the bathroom with ease.

As he stepped into the bathroom, she muttered, "I wondered if you would come."

"Absolutely," he declared, as he propped the crutch against the side of the wall, then, using the handrails, hopped into the shower, and stood behind her. "Do you want me to do your hair?"

"Absolutely. I would love it if you would do my hair."

He gave her scalp a really good scrub, loving the way she leaned back in complete trust, but then why wouldn't she? By the time he was done with her hair, he was having a hard time keeping his own body in control because all he wanted to do was ravage her against the shower wall. He wasn't even sure how well that would work and didn't want to put it to the test. Not right now.

She grabbed the shampoo next and asked, "Do you want me to wash your hair?"

"No, I'm fine," he said. "I'll just shower and then shut this off and come out."

She quickly stepped out, grabbed a nearby towel, and moved into the bedroom, as he finished showering. He joined her a few minutes later, a towel wrapped around his lower body, as he smiled at her.

"I figured you would already be in bed."

"Well, I'm mostly in bed. I'm just sitting here, thinking about the day and all the craziness."

"Of course. I have to admit this entire thing worked out a whole lot better than I thought it would."

"Absolutely," she murmured, "now we just have to make a success out of it."

He sat down beside her. "As far as I'm concerned, this has been a success right from the beginning."

She smiled and nodded. "I can't believe how much *not only my* life has changed but also everyone's lives. You've brought in so much change so quickly."

He frowned and asked, "Is it too quick?"

"No," she said, placing a finger against his lips. "Not too quick. In many ways it was not quick enough." He raised an eyebrow, and she just smiled. "I mean, I'm here. We've got Brian and Scotty, and Killian is coming," she shared, with a bewildered expression. "It is a full-on family for you."

"Not just for me," he corrected, "but for all of us."

"I think that's one of the nicest things. It really does feel as if I'm being included. That wasn't something I ever expected to need or to want, and yet I can't wait for this life. I'm so happy to know that I'm a part of it and a part of everything you have built." She smiled over at him and kissed him gently. "I'm so proud of you."

He pulled her tightly into his arms and muttered, "I'm proud of you."

"I hardly did anything," she noted. "I mean, compared to you, I've done nothing."

"And there is no comparison to be made," he declared. "This isn't a contest. This is all about trying to do the best we can, and that is all we can expect of anybody."

"I love that about you," she whispered. "You always have such an accepting philosophical attitude. Even when I feel shitty about things I've done, you've always been right there, reminding me that I did the best I could in that moment."

"You do … always," he confirmed, with a smile. Then he stood, dropped the towel, and pulled back the bedding, helping her to stand in the meantime. "I don't know about you, but I'm getting tired, and I suspect tomorrow could be just as long as today. A different kind of long but crazy. Hopefully not the same craziness as before though."

"I agree," she murmured, as she curled up on the bed. As he went to lie down, she opened her arms, and he shifted so that he was right there with her.

"We can wait until the morning," he suggested, nuzzling her neck.

"We could, but I suspect that morning will just be a repeat of tonight, and hopefully so many other nights in front of us."

"I always loved that about you," Cage whispered. "You were always right there for everybody."

"Of course," she murmured. "I've got to tell you that being in your arms is like having every day renewed, the best ever, and nothing was quite so nice as being in your arms."

And, with that, he rolled ever so slightly and pulled her into his arms, then laid a kiss on her that held all the pent-up emotional needs he had been holding back, ever since he'd first seen her. When he finally raised his head, she was shuddering in his arms, her eyes glazed over.

"Dear God," she whispered, "I forgot what I'd been missing all these years."

"In that case, I'll spend all of tonight reminding you."

"And you are most welcome to do so," she shared, "but, holy crap, you need to kiss me again." She wrapped her arms around him and pulled him down, so that he was half on her, and his lips were plastered tightly against hers. When he shifted and groaned, she added, "You'll need to do more than this."

He laughed. "And here I thought I would just let you set the pace."

"Oh, you'll let me set the pace all right," she confirmed, "but it's definitely a two-person activity."

And, with that, he lowered his head to explore the body that he loved so desperately, the body that he knew so long ago.

He took a nipple gently into his mouth, suckling deep, feeling her belly curl with the pull, and hearing her whispered groans in his ears. When he moved to the other breast, she was already shaking and shuddering, something he had forgotten. How could he have forgotten that she was so responsive, so joyous in his arms, so completely content to be herself? She had always been that way. It was such a gift, and she never really understood just how it made her so special.

She twisted in his arms, crying out and feeling her body explode, time and time again with his ministrations, until she was exhausted and yet still wanting so much more. She pulled him higher and whispered, "I need you inside me now."

He chuckled. "I forgot how demanding you could be."

"Well, if you think this is demanding, just wait if you don't follow through," she muttered, as she twisted, trying to slide lower beneath him.

When he least expected it, she was suddenly there, her hands wrapped around his erection, and his whole body started to tremble as she moved beneath him. Finally he couldn't handle her wiggling any longer, and he shifted, opening her thighs and plunging deep.

She cried out, twisting in his arms at the sudden possession, and then in a guttural voice whispered, "Don't stop."

Hearing that, he started to move, his body exploding at the joyous reunion with hers, a remembrance of a special moment where they could go back to being who they had always been, lovers of the best kind, both best friends and lovers. When she came apart in his arms again, she held him close, as he finally found his own satisfaction, soon collapsing beside her in her arms.

She whispered, "Now sleep."

"I can do that," he agreed, his voice soft, as he faded. What a lovely way to go into dreamland, and he held her close, kissed her once, and was out.

RISA DRIFTED OFF to sleep beside Cage, absolutely ecstatic at the changes in her life, feeling more fulfilled and happier than she had in eight long years. Now, all she had to do was reap the benefits and enjoy their lives together once more.

With that happy thought, she fell into a deep and silent sleep, absolutely overwhelmed at the beautiful future awaiting her.

EPILOGUE

"We'll have to go visit them," Kat announced to Badger, as she finally put down her phone, still stunned at the turn of events for Cage and Risa. Kat beamed with satisfaction, proud of having guessed it, or for prodding this one into being.

Badger chuckled, shaking his head. "I can't believe that the whole lot of them are together, and even the old man is moving down to join them."

"And yet, why not?" she asked, with a giddy smile. "Being alone is a terrible position to be in."

He caught her head gently between his hands, kissing her, then whispered, "Which is why I am so grateful that you came into my life."

She smiled up at him. "You know I'll never let you forget that, right?"

He burst out laughing. "Yep, I know that, and I think we've done pretty darn well together."

"We have, indeed," she declared. "Now if only I could find some help and some good news for Trey."

"Trey?" Badger asked, staring at her in confusion.

"Yeah, Trey, one of your guys … and now my guy."

He blinked at that and then nodded. "He's relatively new here, so why all of a sudden is he at the top of your concern list?"

"It's not that he's at the top," she clarified, "but he's definitely somebody I want to see happier. I feel as if he's had an awful lot of trauma in his life, so he's due for some good stuff for a change."

"Sure," Badger agreed cautiously, "but we're also talking about finding lost War Dogs, not starting human relationships. Despite the mounting evidence to the contrary, you aren't a matchmaker." When she just smirked at him, he relented. "Okay, so you *are* a matchmaker, but we're really supposed to be doing this for dogs."

She smiled. "If it works out for both, why not? That's perfectly fine with me."

"Sure," he conceded, with an eye roll, "but I don't know how it's happened. I recognize that it has, but we can't expect a love match to happen every time. And, for that matter, I would think you would be all about Timber getting a partner."

"Oh, I think Timber's partner is coming," she said, with a chuckle. "I just don't think he'll recognize it when it happens. How is he doing right now?" she asked, looking over at Badger.

"As far as I know, he's doing just fine. We plan to head out there this weekend and take a look, remember?"

"Yep, I know," she said, "but I still keep thinking about Trey. I was wondering about him for the next job."

"I thought we didn't have any next job," Badger noted.

"Just a couple," she said. "I know you keep thinking that we're done, but they are still trickling in."

"Right. And how much of that trickling in is due to the fact that you keep finding all the dogs and each of the men involved in finding them? And what of Timber? We should be helping him."

"Hey, I'm not the one who's involved to that extent," she pointed out. "That's all you and your guys. I don't know if we have money to send people anywhere, unless I check with you. Besides, we are already helping Timber, and Trey's still on my mind right now."

"Where is this next dog?" Badger asked cautiously. "You know we always try to find the money for expenses on these War Dog jobs. Sometimes it's just easier than others."

"No doubt about that," she agreed, "and this one's in Maine."

"Maine, *huh*? That entails a flight or a drive, maybe of a decent distance. What's in Maine?"

"It's more a case of *who's* in Maine."

"Meaning?"

"This case is one where, chances are, … it's not good news. That's why I'm hesitating about sending Trey out there. I don't want him to feel as if this is a loss, and it could be our first situation where the War Dog is gone for real."

"Explain, please," Badger stated in a sharper tone. "I don't think I've heard about this one."

"Maybe not," she noted. "So, the K9 dog went to its handler, and they were in Maine. He's a fisherman and goes out all the time. Anyway, he got caught in a big storm, and there's been no sign of him."

"Oh, *great*," Badger muttered. "Don't tell me the dog was with him."

"The dog *was* with him, and, of course, as far as the military is concerned, both were lost at sea because nobody has seen any sign of them."

"How long has it been?"

"It hasn't been as long as you might think," she said, looking down at the paperwork. "Three weeks."

"Well, that's long enough. If he's caught out somewhere, three weeks is a long time to try to survive."

"Yes, except the K9 handler was also a survival specialist."

"So, he would have a better chance than most, but—"

"I know," she replied, "and that's why I was a little worried about asking Trey."

Just then somebody poked his head in and greeted them. "Are you talking about me?"

She smiled at him. "Yes, we are. I asked you to come by, didn't I?" She gave Badger a look and continued. "I do have an open opportunity. You know the K9 dogs we've been dealing with?"

Trey nodded. "Yeah, I sure do, and I was wondering if you had one of those jobs that I could do. It's not that I'm *not* happy to help out around here, as I have been. It's just that a War Dog job would make me feel a little more useful."

"What? Roofing doesn't make you feel useful?" Badger teased, with a smile.

"Hey, I'm happy to do any grunt work you have, but tracking down one of these dogs would be something that would always warm my heart."

"And we've had great luck up until now, but the thing is, this case isn't the same as the others."

When she explained it to him, Trey frowned. "Well, if he's lost at sea, there's really nothing I can do."

"I understand," Kat said, "and that's why I was surprised when the War Department asked us, except that both the veteran, who is Silas, and the dog, Schooner, are both survival specialists."

"Ah." Trey nodded, his interest evident from his facial expression. "So, am I looking for the dog or am I looking for the handler … or both?"

"In a case like this, your official job is to look for the dog, but obviously, if you found either or both, we would be ecstatic."

"Right," Trey noted.

"More so because the veteran was out with his daughter, from his first family. She's twenty-four and is also missing. He left behind a second family as well, … and his partner is carrying twins."

"Christ," Trey muttered. "This seems to be a foregone conclusion and could be a very depressing job."

"I know it," she admitted, "which is why I was a bit hesitant to send you."

He nodded slowly. "But"—he stopped for a moment, then nodded—"still better to know, one way or the other, right?"

"It absolutely is better to have that closure, but, if it'll drag you down, it may not be worth it to send you. We don't need you to suffer from any more depression."

He glared, his jaw tightening at her words.

She nodded. "I get it. That's not something you want to hear or to talk about, but I don't want to send you to a job that could trigger you into a downward spiral."

"I already know what I'm diving in to," he pointed out, "and obviously I would do my best to find everybody involved."

"You're a good fit for it," Kat declared, with a smile. "You are definitely uniquely qualified."

He stared at her and smiled. "Don't suppose you saw my file by any chance, did you?"

She gave him a fat smile. "You would be surprised at the things I can find out if I apply myself."

"Right. So, I probably have just as much survival training as they do. Plus, I'm a marine, and I was raised in fishing communities not that far from that region. Do I know the guy?"

"I don't know." Kat pulled out the file. "You tell me. His name is Silas Ragner, and it's his daughter—"

"Missy, … oh my God." He stared at Kat. "It's Missy, Missy Ragner?"

She looked through the file and then nodded. "Yeah, Missy Ragner. Does that make a difference?"

"Just tell me how I'm getting there, and I'll be on my way. Missy Ragner was …" He stopped and smiled. "She's a few years younger than I am, but she was that bright kid on the block, who would go pick flowers and deliver them when you were sick, even though that was the last thing you wanted anybody else to know. She was the girl who just couldn't stop herself from helping people. She was really one of the brightest lights in town."

"Did you know her on a personal level?"

"Outside of being in the same town, no, not really," he said. "I did go to school with her, but she was a few years behind me, but she was always, you know, pretty special." He shrugged. "It would be a huge loss if the community lost her too."

"Well, it sounds as if you need to go find out," Kat noted.

"I would be happy to, and, if I'd known, I would have gone already."

"Exactly. So, in this case, it's the dog and two people."

"What about search and rescue?"

"They gave up," she shared.

He winced. "That bad, *huh*?"

"Rough terrain," she shared, "and I don't have all the details, but you can contact search and rescue as soon as you get there, and they'll have more for you."

"Of course." Trey glanced around, as if already looking to grab his to-go bag.

"So, if this is a yes on your part, we'll arrange a flight and a rental vehicle."

"A flight would be good," he said. "I already have a vehicle available to me. My brother lives there, and I haven't been back in a bit. It's well past time for a visit, but somehow going there was just one more thing on my list that I didn't get around to."

"Now you'll have a chance to take care of that too. Is there any reason not to?"

"No, not at all, and, as a matter of fact, they'll be delighted."

"Good. How about Missy?"

"Missy," he repeated, clearly looking back in time and picturing her for a moment. "Well, if she's still alive and out there struggling to survive, she'll be mad as a hatter. She had good outdoor skills because her dad made sure of it, but that's a long time to be out there."

"Well, they are together hopefully, and the weather's been good," Kat pointed out. "So, if they've managed to get grounded somewhere, you and I both know they have a chance."

"Yeah." Trey turned and headed to the door. "Fly me out tonight, will you?"

"It might have to be tomorrow."

He shook his head. "They don't have time for it to be tomorrow. Get me out tonight." And, with that, he was gone.

This concludes Book 27 of The K9 Files: Cage.

Read about Trey: The K9 Files, Book 28

The K9 Files: Trey (Book #28)

Welcome to the all new K9 Files series reconnecting readers with the unforgettable men from SEALs of Steel in a new series of action packed, page turning romantic suspense that fans have come to expect from USA TODAY Bestselling author Dale Mayer. Pssst… you'll meet other favorite characters from SEALs of Honor and Heroes for Hire too!

A trip home was always in the back of Trey's mind, just with no date set, until he was asked to find a War Dog in his former neck of the woods. He was all about saving the dogs that kept him safe while on tour, so finding out Missy and her father and the War Dog were all missing adds a sense of urgency to the situation.

Missy had gone fishing with her father, as she had done many times before. Not that she was as fishing crazy as he was but just that she loved spending time with her father. What she didn't expect was to end up in a dire situation that had only bad news written all over it.

When Trey found the missing trio, he was overjoyed.

Missy was the same as always—still beautiful even years later. Silas, her father, was in a bad way. Schooner, the War Dog, was the hero of the rescue. Only after getting everyone safely home did Trey realize that this event had been no accident. This was sabotage. And only a few people had access to the equipment, which meant they couldn't trust anyone any longer …

Find Book 28 here!
To find out more visit Dale Mayer's website.
https://geni.us/DMSTrey

Author's Note

Thank you for reading Cage: The K9 Files, Book 27! If you enjoyed the book, please take a moment and leave a short review.

Dear reader,

I love to hear from readers, and you can contact me at my website: www.dalemayer.com or at my Facebook author page. To be informed of new releases and special offers, sign up for my newsletter or follow me on BookBub. And if you are interested in joining Dale Mayer's Reader Group, here is the Facebook sign up page.
http://geni.us/DaleMayerFBGroup

Cheers,
Dale Mayer

About the Author

Dale Mayer is a *USA Today* best-selling author, best known for her SEALs military romances, her Psychic Visions series, and her Lovely Lethal Garden cozy series. Her contemporary romances are raw and full of passion and emotion (Broken But … Mending, Hathaway House series). Her thrillers will keep you guessing (Kate Morgan, By Death series), and her romantic comedies will keep you giggling (*It's a Dog's Life*, a stand-alone novella; and the Broken Protocols series, starring Charming Marvin, the cat).

Dale honors the stories that come to her—and some of them are crazy, break all the rules and cross multiple genres!

To go with her fiction, she also writes nonfiction in many different fields, with books available on résumé writing, companion gardening, and the US mortgage system. All her books are available in print and ebook format.

Connect with Dale Mayer Online

Dale's Website – www.dalemayer.com
Twitter – @DaleMayer
Facebook Page – geni.us/DaleMayerFBFanPage
Facebook Group – geni.us/DaleMayerFBGroup
BookBub – geni.us/DaleMayerBookbub
Instagram – geni.us/DaleMayerInstagram
Goodreads – geni.us/DaleMayerGoodreads
Newsletter – geni.us/DaleNews